CW00725680

HOME FROM HOME

about the author

Susan Price has been writing for as long as she can remember. At fourteen she entered and won the *Daily Mirror* short story competition and at sixteen she wrote *The Devil's Piper*, a fantasy which was published just after she left school. She has now written ten other books, including *From Where I Stand*, *Ghosts at Large*, and most recently a collection of tall tales called *Here Lies Price*.

Apart from writing, Susan has worked as a box-humper in a retail warehouse, a guide in the open air Black Country museum, and for two days as a dish-washer. 'As a dish-washer,' she says, 'I was a complete failure.'

The Ghost Drum won the 1987 Library Association Carnegie Medal for an outstanding children's book.

Home from Home

SUSAN PRICE

faber and faber

LONDON · BOSTON

First published in 1977
by Faber and Faber Limited
3 Queen Square London WC1N 3AU

This paperback edition first published in 1990

Printed in Great Britain by
Cox and Wyman Ltd, Reading, Berkshire
All rights reserved

A CIP record for this book is available
from the British Library
ISBN 0-571-11022-3

To Ginger Preist
And my brother Simon
In return for information rendered

Chapter One

The precinct led from Deal Street to the High Street. It was a long tunnel, partly roofed, lined with shops and paved with pink and yellow squares. A side-junction, mostly taken up with a department store, led to a pedestrian bridge across Deal Street. It was across this side-junction that the stained-glass panel was erected. Much had been made of it when the precinct had first been opened, but now it was patched in many places with plain glass, owing to damage by wind and vandals. But besides a stained-glass window, just where the tunnel channelled the full force of the wind, the architect had also supplied concrete bowls of flowers, and concrete-slab benches, and more pink and yellow tiles to delight the eye.

Two boys came across the foot-bridge on a Saturday afternoon, above the lorries and car-loads of shoppers, down the ramp and into the precinct. In the side-junction it was relatively quiet, and they strolled along, a tall, fair-haired boy, and one much shorter and darker. Ahead of them, in the main part of the precinct, people formed a solid wall.

Then the boys ran into a barrier consisting of one old lady.

"Mike! It is Mike, isn't it?" Little and plump in her black coat and bright-checked head-scarf, she clutched at Mike's arm. "How's your mother?"

The tall boy looked flustered, and rubbed at his hair. "She's —ah—very well, thank you," he said.

"And your father?"

"He's very well, as well," Mike said, with a nervous glance at his friend.

The old lady peered at his friend too. "Oh," she said, "is this Ben?"

"Er—yeah," Mike said.

"Hasn't he grown? Hell—o, Ben. How are *you*, then?"

"Ben" maintained a stony silence, and turned an unblinking stare on Mike.

"Cat got your tongue?" the old lady asked. "Aaah. I've got something for you, I think." She opened her little handbag, and shuffled around at the bottom, finally producing a red and yellow sugar lollipop, which she pushed into "Ben's" hand. "There. Now what do you say?"

"Thank you," Mike said.

"Well, I must catch my bus. 'Bye, Mike. Give my love to your mom and dad."

"G'bye," Mike said, and watched her go all the way to the bridge, rather than turn and face his friend.

"Who was that?" Paul demanded, when he did at last speak.

"I dunno. Might be from where we used to live."

"What you tell her I'm your brother for?" Paul asked, holding his lollipop away from him, like an accusation on a stick.

Mike, half as tall again as Paul, shrank and wriggled before his wrath. "Di'n't mean to. Just sort of came out—I was surprised."

"Huh!" Paul said.

"Well," Mike said soothingly, "you got a lollipop out of it."

Paul almost allowed himself a smile, but controlled it. He shied the lollipop away, and it exploded on the coloured tiles like sugar shrapnel.

"That's a waste," Mike said.

"Oh, sod you," and Paul ran to jump on to the edge of a concrete bowl full of daffodils and hyacinths. He ran along it, see-sawing his arms to keep his balance.

Mike followed at a more sober pace, partly because he was a far more sober personality, but mainly to let Paul cool down. It had put him out, being mistaken for Ben, who was only eleven, nearly five years younger. The thing that really hurt was that, to a short-sighted old lady, Paul could easily pass for an eleven-year-old. He was—tiny was the best way to describe him. He was less than short. Really tiny, and built in proportion, and more hair than he had flesh. Altogether, he resembled a flea.

And now he was staggering up and down the edge of the concrete bowl, back hunched, arms twisted, shouting, "The bells, argh, the bells!" People hurried by, trying to ignore him. "Paul," Mike said, and louder, "Paul. Paul—come on. We'll miss 'em."

"Sod them an' all," Paul shouted, but he jumped down. "Where we meetin' 'em, anyroad?"

"The church," Mike said, and regretted it, for Paul immediately began to sing "All things Bright and Beautiful" off-key and loudly as he shoved through the people on his way to the High Street. Mike trailed behind, trying to look as if he wasn't with him. But at the end of the precinct, Paul turned the wrong way, and Mike had to drop his cover to catch him by the arm and bring him back on the right track. On the walk downhill Paul changed his tune, to "Onward Christian Soldiers". Mike blushed as people passed them with covert glances from beneath their brows, and sly sniggers. Mike would have told Paul to shut up, but knew that any attention, especially of the disapproving sort, would only make him worse. He might go into his impression of James Cagney, or Tarzan, or the fearful fifteen-minute version of Quasimodo, when no one, however complete a stranger, was safe. Paul had no embarrassment when it came to stopping people in the street and asking them if they wanted to buy a vampiric ferret. The only people he was ever shy of were girls and young women—and then, only those he was likely to see again.

Paul stopped singing when the little, seedy church of St Matthew's came into view. Their two friends were waiting on the pavement outside, their backs turned. Paul began to run headlong down the hill, and pounced upon them, slapping his hands on to their shoulders and boosting himself up, well above their heads, nearly knocking them over, landing himself several feet in front of them.

"Oh Jesus, it's him," Tony said.

"Paul—Tormentor! Bloody nuisance," Mal said, brushing at his sleeve, as if Paul had dirtied him. He was all done up in a dark suit, and pale green shirt, while the others were in jackets and jeans. Mal was always full of his own importance.

"What's on then?" Mike asked, sauntering up with his hands in his pockets.

" 'llo Mike," Mal said.

"Orro," Tony said.

"Well, what's on?"

They seemed reluctant to say. "We-e-ll," Mal said.

"*The Exorcist*," Tony admitted.

"*The Exorcist!*" Mike said. "Bloody hell! That place'll be showing silent films next. They drag all the old films round again."

"It's a good film," Mal said placatingly.

Paul shoved in where they had closed ranks to exclude him. "What you on about? *Exorcist?* That's great! My sister saw that when it come round first. Frightened her to death. Let's go and see *The Exorcist*."

"You'd never get in," Mal said crushingly.

"No," Mike said, comforted by this. "They'd never let us in."

"They would," Paul insisted. "They'd let Mal in all right. And you two. . . ."

"And what about you?" Tony inquired.

"Well, 's easy. You and Mal get the tickets for all of us, and I sneak in behind you." Paul beamed at them all.

12

"Oh hark at him," Tony said.

"We wouldn't get in, Paul," Mike said, with a sad, wise shake of the head.

"You don't want to, that's why," Paul said, scraping on the raw truth. He watched them calmly as they winced and reacted.

"What's that supposed to mean?" Tony snapped.

"You'm scared," Paul told him kindly. "That's what it means. You'm scared, scared, scared."

Mal hooted. "Scared—of a film?"

"You am, just the same," Paul said.

"We'm *not* scared—we just wouldn't get in," Mike said.

"You'm scared," Paul said. "You'm all scared. Scared of a film. Scared, scared, scared."

"You're not, of course," Mal said, with a sneer.

"No, I'm not. I'd *like* to go and see it."

"Well, maybe we could get in," Tony said.

Mike and Mal looked doubtful.

"It's probably nothin'," Tony said cheerfully. "'S probably like *Clockwork Orange*. All the fuss an' that in the 'papers, and it was nothin'."

"Yeah, well, I suppose we *could* get in," Mal said, taking up a careless, male-model pose, and sounding very bored.

"No harm in trying," Tony said.

"I don't think they'd let us in, not to *The Exorcist*," Mike mumbled, almost in a whisper.

"Scared," Paul said.

"They'd be bound to let us in," Mal said, tightening the knot of his tie. He looked from one to the other, chin up and very haughty, as if it had been his idea all along. They all moved to join him.

They trooped downhill, and crossed the road to the grubby little picture house, the incredibly unpalatial "Palace". Just inside the swing doors, on the worn smooth orange carpet, they elected Mal ticket-man, and sorted through their pockets for change.

"I owe you twopence then."

"Look—you give me the silver and have the note. . . ."

"Ain't enough."

"Is! Fifty, sixty, seventy. . . ."

"Oh, there's enough. We'll be here all night at this rate. If you need any more, we can give it you."

So they bunched around the ticket office, Mal with his smart suiting and dark moustache pushed well to the front. "Four, please," he said, clattering down the money. And it almost worked. The woman gave them the idlest of glances, but even as her finger moved to trigger the tickets, she spotted a flourish of dark hair on a lower level than the other heads, and craned her neck to see. "Is he with you?" she asked.

They all turned to look down at Paul. He pushed up his chin and said, "Yes, I am," before they had a chance to deny him.

"Sorry, love," said the woman. "I can't let you in."

"Why not?"

The woman tapped the glass of her cubicle next to a notice which said, "No person apparently under the age of eighteen years will be allowed in to see an 'X' film at this cinema." "It's not suitable," the woman added.

"So what? I'm nineteen," Paul said.

The woman gave him a small smile. "Sorry, love." She waited for them to decide what to do. Mal began picking up coins from the counter, to give Paul his money back.

"You going to let them in?" Paul demanded.

The woman gave him a blank look.

" 'Cos you can't, see," Paul said. " 'Cos he's only sixteen—" pointing to Mal, "—and they'm only fifteen."

"Paul, you little bugger," Mike said, betraying himself. He should have looked scornful and laughed it off.

"Are you?" the woman asked.

"No!" Mal said. "He's just saying that because he can't get in."

The woman studied them more closely. "Mmm," she said. "I think you'd all better go."

"But we're eighteen, honest!" Mal said.

"I got my job to think of," said the woman.

Mal and Tony groaned loudly, prepared to go on arguing, but Mike was already sidling out. He'd never really wanted to see the film anyway. Then the nerve of the others broke, and they followed him.

"Sod you, Mentor," Mal said to Paul.

"Yeah, you want your head knocking off," Tony said menacingly.

"Little bahstard," Mal said, copying his father's tone.

"Tormentor," Mike said half-heartedly. He was quite glad that Paul had stopped them getting in.

Paul didn't mind them at all. He'd achieved his aim, to prevent them from seeing a film he couldn't see, and that was all that mattered. He knew that they wouldn't carry out their threats, and he followed them down the steps to the pavement.

"What do we do *now*, then?" Tony asked loudly and disgustedly; adding, "Bloody Mentor."

There wasn't a lot to do. They could wander round the shops, but there wasn't much point, because they hadn't the money to buy anything. They could sit in the park, but that was boring. There were the baths, but they'd have to go home for their swimming things. There was nowhere else to go.

"There's the 'King'," Mike suggested. The "King" was the town's other cinema, a few streets away, and in slightly better repair than the "Palace". No one knew what was on there either, but they decided to walk over and see.

They walked up to the High Street, and along, past the market, and Boots, and Woolworths, through skeins and torrents of people, and prams, and push-chairs, and dogs, and shopping-trolleys, but no cars, because cars were banned from the High Street on Saturdays, and people could stand in the middle of the road to talk. Paul walked the whole way in the road. It gave him a weird sense of freedom and triumph, like a carnival.

A narrow, dark alley ran between a shoe-shop and a solicitor's at the far end of the High Street, and they went down it, tramping over the muddy cobbles and peering into the factory yards that opened off it. The alley led them into Deal Street, and the "King" was just across the road. It was showing *The Sting*.

Paul groaned like wind in the trees.

"What's up with you *now*, bloody Tormentor?" Tony asked.

Mal said, "My brother saw that film in Manchester. He reckoned it was good."

"What? Manchester?" Mike asked.

Paul groaned even more loudly, expressing his opinion of both the film and Mal's brother.

"Oh, shut up, Mentor."

"Nothing ever suits him, that's his trouble," Tony said.

"At least it's a film we can *all* get in to see," Mal said.

Paul seemed to grow suddenly taller. He brushed at his sleeves, as they had all seen Mal do a dozen times that day, but never noticed. "It's such a—bloody—bore," he said, drawling the swear-word in the way Mal had when he wanted to draw attention to something, while seeming to ignore it himself.

Mike laughed outright, so unexpected and perfect was the imitation; Tony was a bit slow. Mal cried, "Mentor!" and they chased across the road to the steps of the "King", running up to the door before Mal gave up with a shaking of fists. Paul knew, and he knew, that all the threats of violence would come to nothing.

Inside they paid their money, and ran in a mob up the stairs into the dark, where the coloured giants dwarfed them. Pushing, shoving, close together, they edged to their seats, careful of the white stripes on the steps; but at last were able to slam down seats and sit down.

Paul found himself in a hostile valley between Tony and Mal. He leaned forward, looking for Mike, who was on Mal's other side, worse and worse.

The film then showing was an educational kind of thing about Hong Kong, with a commentary delivered in a grating style thirty years out of date. Then a news-reel of the same kind—"smoothietone"—and amateurish local advertisements with garish colours and old-fashioned music. Through it all Mike could hear Paul's voice, running in a continuous undertone; imitating the news-reader's tone, parodying his more banal phrases, often predicting very accurately what he would say next: "And talking of . . . but those army boys won't be caught napping . . . As we always say. . . ."

When the film came on Paul insisted on "Da-da-da-da-da-da-da-ing" to the tune, and was hastily silenced with whispered threats and promises. He subsided slowly to watch the film, which was all about con-men and gangsters in the Thirties, laughing easily at the tricks and chases. But Paul stopped laughing when the girl came on. She was supposed to be a waitress in a caff, she was tall and gaunt, with dark hair in an old-fashioned style, and a pale face. The bone above her eyes was deeply shadowed, her cheeks were hollow, she could have been twenty-five or thirty. Mal guffawed and said, "Couldn't he have found something better than *her*," and there seemed to be general agreement. Mike said she was scrawny, Tony that she was old.

But Paul saw something haunting, beautiful—wistful, in her face. He was attracted by her very thinness and paleness. Her eyes seemed full of darkness, and hurt, and compassion.

As it turned out, she was a baddie, and this discovery, with her death, spoilt the film for Paul. He had all the rest to sit through, without her to look out for. He sat glumly, while the heroes triumphed, and refused to laugh at the twist ending. He got up slowly when the others left, following them out with hunched shoulders. He trailed behind them down the stairs, and outside, where he gave up and sank down, in black depression, on the cinema wall.

What did they have to make her a killer for, she was too kind and beautiful, and why couldn't he meet someone like that instead of all the showy wenches there were around, but then, of course, he didn't look like Robert Redford.

Down the road, Mike missed him, and called a halt. "Hey, Paul! Come on."

Paul ignored them. They were boorish and ignorant, and didn't appreciate him, and didn't really want him anyway.

"Paul! Come on! We're going for a drink."

Going for a drink. They only said it to get at him, because they knew he could never get into a pub. It was outside on the steps with a can of shandy and all the neighbourhood's kids. So to Hell with them.

"Aah, to Hell with him," Mal said. Tony silently agreed, and they strolled on down the road. Mike hung back, caught between the two sides. Mal and Tony were right. Paul was often moody and unreasonable, and shouldn't be encouraged.

"Come on, Paul."

Paul felt some small, mean, but warm gratification that Mike had come back to fetch him, proof of his own worth, but it couldn't dispel the misery that filled him. "I don't want to."

"What's up?" Mike asked.

"Nothin'," Paul said. "Nothin's up. I'm just fed up, that's all."

"Well—you seem—miserable, like. 'S why I asked," Mike said uncomfortably.

"I'm just fed up," Paul said.

"Come and have a drink then."

"Oh, sod off!" Paul said, and Mike shrugged.

"All right. If that's the way you want it."

Paul sat and watched as Mike sodded off, running to catch up with the other two. Even though he'd told Mike to go,

Paul felt abandoned. He wondered what to do next, and supposed that there was only home.

He didn't really want to go home, but there was nowhere else, and the bus was waiting, just ready to go out, as if the gods wanted it. So he jumped on and paid his fare, and sulked all the way home. The misery went with him, clamped over his mind, fitting like a tight, irritating skin. The girl in the film had brought it on with her hurt eyes, but it wasn't anything to do with her now. It was a groundless, dragging, pervading, frustrating misery that he couldn't shake off. If he could just name the mood, he could fight it. But it remained stubbornly nameless.

On the doorstep of his home he unbuttoned his jacket, and his shirt collar, to fish out the key that hung about his neck on a piece of string. He had been wearing the key like a necklace since he was seven years old and his mother had gone back to work, and had never broken the habit. He opened the door, and went into the hall, his boot heels clattering on the bare tiles. The hall was so bare that the sound of the door closing echoed. From the living-room came the blaring of a television set.

Paul took off his jacket and hung it up with the other coats. It slid to the floor. So he left it, and went into the living-room. No one looked up or spoke. They knew it was only Paul, and Paul was no novelty.

His mother was sitting with one leg crossed over the other in her armchair, drinking tea and flipping one-handed through a woman's magazine. His father never for a second took his eyes from the "cowboy" on the telly. His elder sister peered into the mirror over the fire, combing her hair and showing her knickers, knock-kneed on her platform soles.

Here it was; the same old thing every day.

The telly in the corner, on its little table; his large father parked ungracefully in the armchair before it. The settee, half-filled with a red plastic washing-basket, overflowing with clothes, and with somebody's coat thrown over the back. The coffee-table, loaded with milk-bottles, cups, plates, bread, sauce, sugar, the teapot, and a vase of daffodils. The ash-tray at his mother's feet. The full clothes-horse that stood on one side of her; the ironing-board, complete with upright iron, that stood on the other; and, beneath the ironing-board, on the floor, his sister's record-player, with a cardboard box holding her records.

Paul went straight to the coffee-table, and felt the teapot. It was still warm and, by tipping it up vertically, he got a cup of tea out of it. He slopped in milk, and drank from the side not stained with lipstick.

Trapped in the small, milky square of the television screen was a moustachioed, shifty-eyed man in a black hat, obviously a baddie. Hiding behind a cactus, the baddie fired off several shots at his pursuers, before his gun clicked on an empty barrel. Mouthing an oath, he hurled the gun at them instead.

"We've got the goddurned, ornery, no-good rattlesnake now!" cried the grizzled old-timer, slapping his fist into his palm.

Paul turned away. "Mom. Mom. Mom." He went in to low-power first gear, grinding like a cement mixer. "*Moth*—er, *Moth*—er."

Mrs Mentor looked up from her magazine. She was an attractive woman, her hair tinted, her make-up in style. "What?" she said.

Paul was irritated by her complacency and coolness. "Anything to *eat*?" he said.

"Didn't you have no chips nor nothin'?"

God give me strength. "No, or I wouldn't be askin', would I?"

His mother sighed, put down her cup and dropped her magazine beside it on the floor. In her turn, she began calling. "Horace. Horace. Horace, I'm talking to you. Horace."

And Kath took it up. "Dad. Dad. Mom wants you, Dad. Dad."

"Horace!"

"You'll never take me alive, Sheriff!"

"Horace! Horace!"

"I'm a-comin' in, McKighy. You're a-goin' to pay for that old man's life."

"Dad."

Oh Lord, Paul thought. Wish I'd never spoke now.

"What?" Mr Mentor cried, starting suddenly and looking wildly round.

"Do you want something to eat?" Mrs Mentor asked.

"Oh. Ar. Wouldn't mind."

"What d'you want then?"

"Eh?"

"I said—what d'you want then?"

Mr Mentor thought for a while. "What is there?"

Paul sighed, but he was powerless to stop the machinery he had set in motion.

Mrs Mentor cast her eyes to the ceiling. "Well—there's a tin of tuna fish—you could have some sandwiches of that. Or I could boil you an egg. You could have some egg sandwiches if you like. Or toast. Baked beans on toast, we got some of them. Got some brown bread an' all if you'd like that. Or we could send Paul for some faggots. Or chips."

"Oh—I dunno," Mr Mentor said.

"Tuna sandwiches'd be easiest," Mrs Mentor said hopefully. She was very tired.

Mr Mentor roused himself on one elbow. "Got no boiled ham?"

"That was yesterday, you fool."

"The faggots, I think," Mr Mentor said.

"Paul—fetch my purse, there's a love——"

"I ain't fetchin' nothin'," Paul said, sitting down on the settee with a thump.

"Oh!" said his mother, in ominous tones.

His father eyed him coldly. "Well! We'll have nothin'

then." And, leaning forward, he turned up the volume again.

Paul went into the kitchen and, from the clutter of tins in the pantry, found the tuna fish. He opened the can and took it back into the living-room. Using one of the knives from the breakfast plates on the table, he began to make himself sandwiches.

"Oh," said his mother, from behind her magazine, "some people make free, don't they?"

But that was all she said, because it was too much trouble even to nag him. She hadn't long got in from work.

Kath went out and Paul ate his sandwiches, staring at rather than watching the television. The next happening was Mr Mentor's silent arising, on his way to the pub. The cowboy had given way to a quiz-game and Paul decided he'd had enough. He went into the front room.

The front room was a communal rubbish-dump. Anything unneeded, or unused, was thrown into it. There was a vacuum-cleaner, and piles of unironed washing, spare blankets, waste-paper, old toys, coats, rags (to be thrown out, one day) a rolled-up rug, an empty fish-tank, broken ornaments (to be mended, one day) a defeated armchair, an old mattress, a set of kitchen shelves, and many, many things that had been buried and forgotten. Balanced on top of an old pram was Paul's school bag, and inside it was the book Mr Trevors had given him to read. A book of short stories by a man named Ray Bradbury. "Good book," Mr Trevors had said. "Science fiction. You read it and let me know what you think of it, because I'd like your opinion." A touch of child-psychology which Paul had not missed. Still, it was better than watching the telly.

Back in the living-room, he sat curled up by the basket of washing, and studied the cover. It was silver, with strange flying beasts, and comets. Just the kind of thing he liked to paint himself, at school, in the art lesson. Science fiction books always had good covers. He spent hours looking at them in bookshops.

He opened the book and read first the title, then the author's name, and then the date of publication. He was a little afraid to start it, in case he was disappointed, or in case it was too difficult.

"What's that?" his mother asked. "Got your nose stuck in a book again?" And when Paul ignored her, "I'm talking to you, young man. Are you too ignorant to answer me?"

"Yes," Paul said, hissing it between his teeth, "I have got my nose stuck in a book again."

"What is it this time?"

"I dunno," Paul said.

His mother seemed to find nothing unusual in this. She threw her magazine on the floor, and said, with lackadaisical concern, "You'll ruin your eyes with all that reading. You will."

Paul unfolded his legs, distracted and irritated by her interruptions. "Least they won't go square," he said.

Mrs Mentor's eyes narrowed. "Are you being cheeky, young man?"

"Yes," Paul said.

His mother laughed, took a drag and blew smoke at the ceiling. "You'm honest, I'll give you that. But you will, you'll ruin your eyes." When she spoke again, humour deepened her voice, betraying her joke. "You'll addle your brains."

Paul sat very still, and fixed her with a cold, hostile stare. He hoped, in this way, to so offend her that she wouldn't speak to him again.

She looked back at him through the smoke of her cigarette, her expression indifferent. "You'm a funny little whatsit, ain't you?" she said. "Never see hide nor hair of you all day, and when you'm in all you want to do is read."

Paul stirred uncomfortably, and broke the stare, looking down at the book. "What else is there?"

"Well—you could talk to me, for one," Mrs Mentor said, and she crossed her legs, and waited hopefully. "What you been doin'?"

Paul felt her waiting, and waiting, and waiting—his eyes backtracked, reading over and over the book's first sentence.

To break the waiting, he said, "Talk to you? Huh."

Mrs Mentor laughed with a hard sound. "Thanks muchly. If that's the way you feel about my company, I'll go and make a cup of tea." Her stockings and skirt swished across the room; she paused at the door in a haze of the deep scent she always wore. "I daresay you'll be glad to drink the tea when I've made it."

Paul shrugged her off with his guilt when he heard the door close behind him. By the time she came back, he had managed to entrench himself so deeply in the dream-like world of monsters and flying machines that the book held, that she was unable to reach him.

And he didn't drink any of the tea.

Chapter Two

The last lesson on Monday afternoon was a free lesson for Paul's form. In the Headmaster's theory, this meant a quiet period for doing homework, inwardly digesting notes, revising, learning—and marking for the teachers. In practice, it meant a quiet period for holding a card-school, chatting up girls, talking, fighting—and a headache for the teachers.

Paul had shaken off the doldrums of the weekend, and was playing a kind of tennis with Tony, where they knocked a crumpled ball of paper from one to another with text-books. Paul used *Diggory's Illustrated History*, published 1925, which made a large bat, while Tony preferred a more difficult game with *Longstreet's Mathematics*, a slim, ink-marked volume. The court was the whole room, including chairs and desks, with Paul making especial use of these, since his height put him at a disadvantage. In jumping across the aisles, he rocked the desks, and nearly knocked them over; he trampled books and scattered pencils, made girls scream raucously in annoyance, and more than once fell heavily to the ground. But all this was what put the game above ordinary tennis.

The teacher, well known for being weak, sat at his desk, buried in his marking. The noise level had crept up without his noticing, and although he was dimly aware of the tennis game, he preferred to ignore it rather than make the effort to stop it. He knew that Mentor was lurking somewhere in this class, and he dreaded Mentor, because the little swine always gave you a dozen words for one over any order or request, whether it concerned him or not. He was a trouble-maker, pure and simple, no matter what other teachers might say about his talent or intelligence.

Then the door opened. There was immediate silence, and Paul dropped from the desk he was standing on into the aisle, scooping up the fallen ball of paper.

Mr Trevors came in, a tall man with square, black-framed spectacles. He had a word with their teacher, and then came up the aisle, shouting above the rising chatter, "Mentor! Paul—I'd like a word with you."

Paul was sitting on Mike's desk. He had given the ball of paper to Mike, who had stuffed it into his pocket. Paul now had *Diggory's Illustrated History* open and looked entirely innocent. "Yes, sir?"

"I want some volunteers," Mr Trevors said. Tony and Mike exchanged sardonic glances; Paul laughed.

"For our 'Active Christians' group," the teacher explained.

"I'm an atheist," Paul said promptly.

Mr Trevors drew an empty chair into the aisle and sat down on it, his head on a level with Paul's. "So'm I," he said, "but the Active Christians do a lot of good work—I mean, really *worthwhile* work," he added hastily, at the looks on their faces. "And Mr Archer wants some volunteers, and I said I'd help him."

Paul shrugged, threw Mike's rubber in the air, and caught it. "We don't like that sort of thing," Mike said, speaking for them all.

"Why not?" the teacher asked, and Mike flushed, and looked down.

" 'S hypocritical," Paul said, as if this was obvious.

The teacher gave a big grin, to show them how very wrong they were, and said, "You don't have to pray or anything. You don't even have to be Christian. You don't have to be Christian to do good worthwhile work, do you?"

"Go and ask the Sixth Form," Paul said. "Everybody's always telling us what a good example they are. Or do the worthwhile work yourself."

Mr Trevors's cheery good humour crumpled for a second, but he pulled it back together. "I *have* asked the Sixth Form, *and* I've got some volunteers from them. And I reckon I do enough good work teaching you apathetic lot. Come on, Paul —helping the aged. Weeding gardens and painting kitchens is better than hanging around pub car parks."

"Depends on your tastes," Paul said.

"Mike?" Mr Trevors asked, but Mike shifted in his seat and stared out of the window, refusing to give a straight "No".

"Tony?"

"I haven't got the time," Tony said blandly.

Mr Trevors sighed, leaned back and crossed his legs. "Oh well—d'you like that book, Paul?"

Paul's eyes jumped up to the teacher's. He knew what this was. " 'S all right," he said. "Not bad."

"Oh good, I thought you might enjoy it. I've got a lot more like that. . . . Oh well, I suppose I'll have to go back to Mr Archer and tell him I've failed."

"You've got some from the Sixth Form, you said," Paul put in quickly.

"Yes, but Mr Archer was hoping to see each form represented, you see."

Paul sat on the desk, throwing the rubber from hand to hand; the teacher sat on the chair in the aisle, and each waited for the other to weaken.

But all the weight was on Mr Trevors's side. Paul was being reminded of all the favours the teacher had done him, the books loaned, and the records; the time Mr Trevors had got him on to a Third Year trip to the Birmingham Rep to see *Macbeth*. Paul had gone for the outing, but had enormously enjoyed the play, which was like a mixture of the horror film on a Friday night, and a pantomime. He was obliged to the teacher.

He was also being blackmailed. If he put Mr Trevors out, then there wouldn't be any more loans of books, or records, and no more wangling to get him included on trips he wasn't entitled to. There wouldn't be any more long, idle, after-school chats, when Paul went to borrow or return books, about Mr Trevors's home in Leeds, and about his father, by all accounts a sharp, self-educated man, who could still teach his teacher son a thing or two; and about obscure points of History, such as Atlantis: Reality or Myth?, and where the Vikings came from before they came from Scandinavia. Paul didn't contribute much to these talks, but he was—had been—a fascinated listener, held as much by Mr Trevors's lung-power as by what he was saying.

And really—it was the truth, he wasn't losing much by spending his spare time 'helping the aged'. Home. The life-wastage in watching films inside dark, hot cinemas. The long, aimless ramblings around the streets at night. The girl-chasing that never came to anything because he didn't look like Robert Redford, and was, secretly, terrified of girls, young and pretty girls, anyway.

"All right," he said. "You can put my name down."

"Great!" Mr Trevors said, and produced a pen, and a folded piece of paper from his pocket, leaning it on his knee to write. "Paul Men-tor. Mike, how about you?"

Mike sighed. He thought he'd got out of answering.

"Go on, Mike," Paul said. He wanted support in this new venture.

"I dunno," Mike said.

"Go on," Paul urged. "You've nothin' else to do."

Between Paul's urging and the teacher's eyes, Mike gave in. "All right. Go on."

"I know, what about me?" Tony said. "O.K. Go on. You can put me down for a night or so."

"That's great, lads," Mr Trevors said. "Thanks very much, I knew you'd come across. They hold the meetings Monday and Thursday, after school, so I'll tell you what to do—skip tonight and come Thursday. It starts at half five, but they have a prayer meeting or something, so I shouldn't come until six, and Mr Archer'll tell you what to do."

"Where?" Paul asked.

"Where? Oh! Room 36; room 36, Thursday, six o'clock. Right?" Half-way down the aisle, he turned and called, "Oh Paul! I've got this book you might like to borrow when you've finished the other . . . ?"

Paul nodded and laughed.

When Trevors had gone, Tony said, "Another fine mess you've got us into."

"I dunno," Paul said. "It might be all right. Can give it a try."

"Oh yeah. A real riot of fun, I don't think."

"Well, if you don't like it, you can chuck it up, can't you?" Paul said.

"Oh ar? An' what about Trevors?"

Paul laughed. "Sod him." He slid off the desk and took the ball of paper from Mike's pocket, batted it into the air. Tony leapt to knock it back.

On Wednesday night, while he put on his jacket to go and call on Mike, Paul shouted to his mother, "Mom! Mom! I might not be in when you get back tomorrow."

"When are you?" his mother asked. "I never see you. Pass me me fakes off the shelf, will you, there's a love?"

Paul took the cigarettes and matches from the shelf and passed them to her.

"Where are you going then, that you bother to tell me about it?" Mrs Mentor asked, around her cigarette as she lit a match.

"Just out with Mike and Tone," Paul said. She gave him

back the cigarettes and matches, and his father silently held out his hand. Paul passed the cigarettes to him.

"And where you off to tonight?"

"I dunno. Out with Mike," Paul said.

"That's all right then," Mrs Mentor said. "Just so long as I know where you are."

"Ah, the new boys," Mr Archer said, as he oozed over to them. He was a tall, blond, angular Maths teacher with religious convictions. "Now you're Paul——"

"Paul Mentor."

"Mike Preston."

"Anthony Hill."

"Good, good. Yes." The Active Christians milled about, talking and scuffling, collecting bags and coats to leave. "I've got it all sorted out," Mr Archer said. "Tony—you go with Peter here." Peter was a tall, sombre-looking second-sixth-former. "He's been visiting our old folk for nearly two years now, haven't you, Peter. He'll look after you." Peter and Tony looked at each other with instant dislike, and slowly moved away. "Now—Paul and Mike, you have quite an adventure. Someone we've never visited before, so you'll all be starting off quite fresh. Don't worry though, I shall be coming with you the first two or three visits, to break the ice —and then you'll be on your own, unless you want help. Happy?"

"Yessir," Mike said, since Paul didn't make any attempt to answer. Paul was watching Mr Archer raptly, and Mike guessed that the teacher would soon be included in his repertoire along with the Queen and Quasimodo.

"Come along then," Mr Archer said, "I'll give you a lift." As they followed him, Paul began to walk like him, mincing and wiggling his fingers, until Mike shoved him in the back. Mike was afraid the teacher would turn around.

Mike sat in the passenger seat of the car, while Paul leaned over the back. "Mrs Maxwell really needs a little help around the house," Mr Archer said. "She has rheumatism, you see, and can't get about much. She used to have a grandson—she'd brought him up, but—a great shame—he was killed in an accident some two years ago now, I believe. She has had a tragic life, really, she's been terribly unlucky with her family. Terribly unlucky."

"Aah. Shame," Paul said, dead-pan.

Mike flinched. He knew that Paul always said this sort of thing when people told him sob-stories. It meant no more than "bless you" when someone sneezes. But no doubt Mr Archer thought him a callous little——

"The Vicar thinks she would enjoy some young company. It was he who talked her into allowing some of our Active Christians to visit."

Mike said nothing, because he was feeling very out-of-place, sitting with an Active Christian, speeding up the road on a do-gooding expedition. Paul was silent for a while, resting his hands and chin on the backs of the front seats, and then said, "Shouldn't you send her two who'm more—like, experienced?"

"Oh, there's not much experience necessary," Mr Archer said. "The work that's to be done is very elementary—sweeping floors, washing-up—anyone could do it, even me." He laughed at this. "What means much more is warmth and friendliness, and willingness to help. It means a lot to old folk, you know, a friendly face."

And "young folk" Paul thought. Why segregate old people like that? Anyway, the friendly faces probably meant nothing more to them than an intrusion.

Mrs Maxwell lived in a street of very old houses, all built of narrow bricks, blackened with dirt. Both the windows and the doors were very small. They left the car, and Mr Archer knocked on the door. "Come in," someone called.

Mr Archer opened the door and went in, bending almost double to fold his height through the tiny opening. Mike, behind him, ducked too. Only Paul could walk through upright.

The street door opened directly into the house's living-room. It was not large, and it was crowded. Over it all there seemed to be a yellow dust, or some sort of yellowish, transparent, protective cover. The place smelt of old things, preserved, but fading away.

The fire was in an old range, and on either side of the fire was an armchair. The middle of the room was filled by a big square table. Behind the door, under the window, was a sideboard, of a ponderous size. Straight-backed chairs and stools were everywhere, filling all the spaces left over by the larger pieces of furniture.

Mr Archer stooped over the armchair that had its back to the door, and said, "It's only me, Mrs Maxwell. How are you? Good, good. I've brought two young men with me, they're going to be a great help."

Paul, wandering around Mr Archer, came face to face with the old lady in the armchair. She looked like a teddy-bear. Small and plump; a round, timid face, with round, thick spectacles balanced on a round bump of a nose; her arms all bundled up in a tartan cloth, or shawl, or something, her skirt black and over-long, her feet strange in red fluffy slippers. He smiled at her, for lack of anything to say, but she didn't smile back.

"I don't know what they can do," she said to Mr Archer, looking dubiously at Paul.

"Anything you want them to, Mrs Maxwell. They're strong and willing and very bright."

"There ain't nothin' *for* 'em to do," said the old lady.

"Well, we'll see about that, Mrs Maxwell. This is—er—Paul—Paul Mentor; and this is his friend, Michael."

"Hello, Mrs Maxwell," Paul said, and Mike nodded. The old lady didn't seem to know what to make of them.

"You can switch me radio on," she said suddenly. The radio stood on the corner of the table. Paul, being nearest, switched it on. "What station do you want?" he asked.

"Any one'll do."

So Paul turned it until he found some music being played on violins and whatnot, which he thought suitable for old ladies.

"That's better," Mrs Maxwell said. "I like to hear the radio."

"And Mike," Mr Archer said, "will put the kettle on. Through there, Mike." Mike was waved through a door at the far end of the room, looking back hesitantly, and Mr Archer settled to a chat with Mrs Maxwell.

Paul slipped through the door after Mike. It opened on to a brew-house, or wash-house, or even scullery; really an extension built to house a gas-stove and sink. There was a dresser too, and a work-surface along one wall. It was a badly built place; it must rain in, because the stove was going rusty, and all the walls were damp. The floor was covered with worn lino, which nearly tripped Mike up, let alone Mrs Maxwell. Paul felt about the clammy walls until he found the light switch, and switched on an unshaded light-bulb, hanging from the ceiling on a long flex, which was almost worse than no light at all, because it threw confusing shadows.

The kettle—rusty—was on the stove, and Mike filled it at the sink, set it on the gas-ring. He found a slightly damp box of matches on the work-surface, and, after two or three attempts, succeeded in striking one, and lighting the gas. Paul, meanwhile, had opened the far door and was looking out on to the yard, a long narrow stretch of earth, with a herring-bone path, and a shed which was the outside lavatory.

"Now we'll have to find the milk and sugar and cups and saucers," Mike said plaintively.

Paul shut the yard-door and, with the practice of long experience, turned the dresser inside out in a couple of minutes, and could have given a list of its contents. In its bottom cupboards he found the milk and the sugar; also the tea and bread and all that had to be stored; and by pulling the drawers out and climbing up them, found the cups and saucers and all the crockery in the top cupboards. He set out four cups and saucers on the tin tray he found lodged behind the sink taps.

"Should we?" asked Mike.

"Should we what?"

"Put cups for ourselves?"

" 'Course! We'm guests, ain't we? I wonder how she gets the crockery up there?"

Mike opened the tea-caddy, and found a spoon inside. It was wildly decorated with metal curls and spirals, and inscribed, "A present from Loch Lomond". He carefully measured five spoons into the pot.

"The ladder," Paul said, from behind him.

"Eh?"

"She climbs up the ladder," Paul said. He pointed to a set of step-ladders leaning behind the yard-door. "The silly old fool."

When they took the tea into the next room, Mr Archer and the old lady were still talking, or rather, Mr Archer was. Mike stood by the table and tried to look intelligent, but Paul took no notice of the conversation at all.

He studied, instead, the range. He had never seen one before. It was set back into the wall, and the fire was in a little grate between two square hobs. Everywhere, raised up, were patterns of hearts and flowers.

The table had three cloths. On top, a checked plastic one, beneath that, a linen one, and on the bottom a heavy, fringed, velvet cloth in a deep tawny orange colour. Paul dropped on his knees to crawl underneath the table and peer out through the fringes. Mike saw him, and flushed with embarrassment, but neither the teacher nor the old lady noticed. Out from under, Paul yanked open the drawer of the sideboard, finding the cutlery inside. He took some teaspoons to the table. The door beside the sideboard proved to be the coal-house, and the door further along in the same wall opened on to stairs which led steeply upwards into darkness. It was all very interesting, being let loose in someone else's house.

"So," Mr Archer was saying, "one of the boys will get your shopping on Saturday. Which shall it be? Boys?"

Mike didn't answer, but Paul, turning from the staircase, said, "I will, Mrs Maxwell."

Mike stared at him resentfully, but couldn't say anything with Mr Archer there. On Saturdays they *always* went out looking for things to do. Paul smiled at him.

"And sir, if Mrs Maxwell don't mind," he said, "we could get that lino up in the kitchen. It's dangerous. She could fall over."

"But—it keeps the floor warm," Mrs Maxwell said, horrified at this threat to her home.

"I can get you a rug," Paul said. "Do you want a cup of tea?"

Chapter Three

"Paul," said his mother on the Saturday morning.

He looked up from his cornflakes. She'd started out on her way to the front door once, and he hadn't expected her to come back. "What?"

"Where's that rug gone that was in your bedroom?"

"What rug?"

"You know what rug. That old brown one."

"I dunno. Never noticed it was gone."

"Well, it is. Disappeared."

"I dunno where it is," Paul said.

"Oh well—I shall be late for work if I don't hurry up. 'Bye, love. Look after yourself won't you now?"

"Goodbye," Paul said.

He heard the door slam behind her, and then the house was very quiet. Even the telly was silent, on its table in the corner. There came mysterious creaks and buzzings.

The last cornflake eaten, the last spoon of milk scooped up, he wedged the bowl on to the coffee-table, making a space for it amongst the cups and milk-bottles, cereal packets and plates. He found his shirt from the jumble on the settee, and put it on, returned to search for his jumper. It was his Saturday jumper, purple with a white chevron, and he had put it on the night before to celebrate the weekend.

His shoes had crawled under his father's armchair, and he had to lie flat to fish them out, sitting in the chair to put them on. Under his father's bulk the chair had spread and flattened, and grown hopeless. If Paul sat right back in it, he was dwarfed by the back and sides, and almost sucked under the cushion. It was like sitting on a hungry jelly-fish.

Dressed, he turned down the gas-fire and shut the living-room door after him, checked that the back door was locked. His jacket was thrown across the old pram in the front room. He put it on, then remembered the rug, which he'd hidden in a drawer, and ran upstairs to fetch it. He rolled it into a dusty, musty tube and tucked it under his arm.

He did not take the most direct way to Mrs Maxwell's, because he did not want to meet any of his friends, or any of his mother's friends, but his family were early risers and he got out of his own district without seeing anyone he knew.

He did wonder if Mrs Maxwell would be up yet, but by the time he reached her street it was nearly a quarter past nine, so she was bound to be. Old people were usually early risers too.

At Mrs Maxwell's door he knocked and called out, "It's Paul," then went in. The old lady was up and dressed, and sitting very stately in the armchair with its back to the door. There was no fire in the range for all it was rather a cold morning.

Paul went around her chair and said, "Hello. It's me again." For all he had visited her on Thursday, he felt a little shy. He felt guilty because he knew he came for the thrill of being let loose in a strange house more than to help the old lady.

Mrs Maxwell looked at him as if she didn't recognize him, and said, " 'Lo, love."

Paul stood the rolled rug on its end and said, "I've brought you a rug for your kitchen." She didn't answer him, and he was quick to explain, "Me Mom didn't want it, but it's a good rug, so I brought it you."

The old lady gazed abstractedly through him, so he laid the rug down, shrugged uncomfortably, and said, "Well—anything I can do?"

"I dunno," the old lady said. It was obvious that she didn't want to ask him to do anything.

Paul felt more confident at this. "That's what I've come for, to help you. Shall I make a fire?"

"You could do that," she said, grudgingly.

Paul studied the old range. He had made fires before, but never in a contraption like that.

"You'll have to get the ess out first," she said. "That's the ess-hole down there."

Ash, she meant. He picked up a shovel from the hearth, then put it down again and went to look for the ash-bucket. He found it by the yard-door in the kitchen, and brought it back, tipping the ashes from the pan into it.

"You'll find some kindling and paper in the coal-hole," said the old lady, sitting bundled in her shawl.

Steps led down into the damp, dark coal-hole. Paul felt along the spider-webbed wall for the light, and was then able to find the thin sticks of kindling and the piles of old newspapers. He laid balls of paper in the grate, with wigwams of sticks over them, and one or two pieces of coal. The old lady looked on, sleepily, but with approval. Paul went to search the kitchen for the matches.

He began the old, frustrating game of trying to get a fire to burn. Time and time again the paper would burn away before the wood or coal had caught. "They tell you, be careful, a spark'll start a fire," Mrs Maxwell said. "I never believed it meself." But at last she said, speaking as an expert, "Leave it now; it'll burn up."

"Whew!" Paul said, looking at his coal-blackened hands. "It'll be a bit warmer anyway."

"Mmm, it was cold," she said dreamily. "But me hands hurt this morning."

Paul looked, but her hands were wrapped up in her shawl. "What's wrong with 'em?"

"Rheumatism or summat saft."

"Oh, yes," Paul said. He didn't really know what it was, although he'd heard of it dozens of times before.

"Some days it's worse than others," the old lady said. "I couldn't face making a fire this morning."

Paul knelt on the hearth, looking up into her creased, powdery, vague face; wondering. "Why not?" he asked.

Mrs Maxwell pushed one hand from beneath her shawl. It was as skinny and fragile-seeming as a leaf, with the bones showing. All the knuckles were swollen and shiny, and some of the fingers went off at odd angles. "It hurts to move 'em, love."

"Oh," said Paul, studying the hands. And a second later, "You've had no breakfast then?"

"No."

"What d'you want? I'll make it, that's what I come for."

"I never have breakfast. Never have done, all me life."

"Oh—What about a cup of tea then?"

She nodded absently. "Be nice."

Paul took the matches from the table and went into the kitchen. Then he left the matches in the kitchen and went back and collected the rug that he had left lying on the floor. He laid it down on the worst part of the kitchen floor, and it covered up the torn lino for the time being, but the lino really wanted getting up altogether.

He set about making the pot of tea. As he moved from tap to stove, to cupboard, he noticed how often his hands opened, fisted, flexed. He thought how it would be if they hurt each time. And of everything else to be done about the house that would call up that pain. He felt guilty again, even though he hadn't created rheumatism.

He went to the door of the living-room, and said, "I'll come in the morning and make you a fire."

"No need, love," Mrs Maxwell said, as if half-asleep.

There it was. She didn't want him there. He was an intruder.

Bloody-mindedness took over. Right then. He'd come to-morrow and every morning. Now he'd go and make the tea.

He brought the teapot to the table and, while it was brewing, poked the fire to try and get some life out of it. "You stay in bed tomorrow till I come and make a fire," he said, but she appeared not to be listening. So he poured her a cup of the tea, and she took it between both hands, without bending her fingers.

Paul wandered into the kitchen and did something he'd meant to do Thursday. He climbed up and took all the crockery from the top cupboards and stacked all the cups, plates and dishes at the back of the dresser. The step-ladders he humped down the yard and slid in beside the outdoor lavatory.

He felt a great relief now that Mrs Maxwell couldn't climb up her step-ladders and fall off. Or, at least, would find it very difficult. News could come through of scores of old ladies crashing from step-ladders and leave him cold. But now he knew Mrs Maxwell, and that made it different. Besides, he felt a kind of responsibility. It was easy to ignore something you knew nothing of, but impossible to comfortably ignore anything once you were conscious of it.

When he went back inside, Mrs Maxwell was still in her chair, still holding her teacup, and he was glad to see that the fire had burnt up. Her hazy eyes caught sight of him in the doorway. "Oh," she said, "I thought you'd gone home."

"No," he said. "I've been moving your dishes and that out of the top cupboard. It's dangerous like that, I thought—I——" Paul suddenly saw that he couldn't finish the sentence without being insulting. What did it matter what he thought? What was he going to say, call her stupid? It wasn't his house, he had no right or business to move her things about.

"I always kept me crockery in that top cupboard," Mrs Maxwell said. "Kept it safe from the childer, and then the dust off."

Paul flushed and twisted, guilty and hurt.

The old lady smiled slowly. "I always been meaning to move 'em."

Paul watched her closely before he realised she was teasing him, and grinned nervously. He hadn't thought her capable of joking, you didn't think of it with so old a lady. He came into the room and felt the teapot. It was still warm. "D'you want another cup of tea?"

"No," she said. And then, "You have one if you want, my love."

But that wouldn't do. The admission fee to this place was work, and he cast around for some work to do. "Shall I wash up?"

She smiled secretively. "There's only that cup. Only needs swilling under tap."

"I know," Paul said, "I'll break you up some wood." He went back down into the coal-hole. Several orange-crates and apple-boxes provided the kindling, but first they had to be broken up. Paul stomped them and banged them against the walls, rended them apart with his bare hands, Tarzan of the Budgies. But he kept one box back, lining it with old news-paper and filling it with coal and wood. He heaved it up the stairs and across the room, dropped it thankfully by the hearth. The old lady looked on, dully, without expression.

"That's so you won't have to keep fetching coal from down there," he explained.

"Hmm," she said. The clock on the mantelpiece ticked loudly and slowly.

Paul stood up, wiping his brow, and looking for something else to do. "Well——"

"Oh Lord!" said the old lady, tossing up a corner of her shawl pettishly, "it's like having a buzzy-fly about the place. Sit *down* for a minute and be restful."

Paul grinned and sat down on a little square stool with a raffia seat. "Anything you want me to do, I'll do it," he said, and was then afraid she would tell him to go home. "Clean up —sweep—anything."

"You just sit there, and I'll know where you am and what you'm doin'. What's your name?"

Paul was surprised. He'd told her his name at least twice. "Paul Mentor."

"Paul Mentor," she repeated, and was quiet for a long time.

"All they do for old folk these days," she said suddenly. "Sending folk round to see 'em. Saftness."

This wasn't encouraging, but Paul was determined. "Do you want any shopping done?" he asked doggedly. "That's what I really come for, to do your shopping."

"I can do me shopping meself, thank you. I have every other week."

Paul took that as a slap in the face. But he kept on trying. "I could help. I could carry your bag. And reach things for you. And help—help with the prices."

The old lady pulled her shawl around her and brooded on the unfairness of the world which had conspired against her; to rob her of her family, confuse her, frighten her, leave her lonely and weak. Help was all very well, but when it was handed to you on a plate, how could you trust it? These young lads today . . . but still . . . she wouldn't shame herself by agreeing or asking—just let it go, and if he was still around when she went to the shops, she supposed he would come too.

But she wasn't ready to go yet. Paul had to wait. He waited from ten in the morning until two in the afternoon. He was unusually patient, even though the hours weighed heavily in that quiet, still-aired place. Mrs Maxwell didn't speak, seemed to be day-dreaming, and he didn't want to disturb her. He moved about quietly, washed the cup she'd used and emptied her teapot on to her patch of garden in the yard. He shook the cloth, which didn't need shaking, straightened the rug over the lino, tidied up the tidy kitchen—all for something to do, so that he could feel useful and not nosey.

The one really useful thing he could have done, he missed. At about eleven o'clock, Mrs Maxwell suddenly rose with creaks and gasps from her chair and went into the kitchen. She came back with a packet of crisps, sat down again and ate them slowly, one by one, as if he wasn't there. She obviously didn't believe in talking with her mouth full, and she didn't speak for a long time after she had crumpled the packet and thrown it into the fire.

So suddenly that he jumped, she asked, "What time is it?"

Paul became aware again of the loud ticking of a clock, but out of habit looked at his watch. "Ten past two—nearly quarter past."

The old lady groaned and made to heave herself out of her chair, then sank back. "Make yourself useful," she said. "Go and fetch my coat."

"Where is it?"

"Behind the door in the kitchen."

Paul fetched the coat, a long, thick black affair which was surprisingly heavy when hung over his arm. He wondered how Mrs Maxwell could walk in it. Hanging on the same hook as the coat were two shopping bags, and he took them both into the other room.

Mrs Maxwell hooted. "How much d'you suppose I'm going to buy? You can leave one of them behind, my lad."

Paul dropped both bags as she started to get up, and took her arm to help her. And when she was up, he spread her coat to help her into it.

"A little gentleman, aren't you?" she said, and he couldn't tell if it was praise or sarcasm. Praise, he supposed, since it was an old-fashioned sort of sentiment, and she didn't seem a sarcastic person.

"I'll fasten the buttons for you," he said, nipping round her, remembering her rheumatism.

"I can manage meself, thank you," she said quickly, but he was already wrestling with the first big button and the stiff material. And it did hurt, to fasten buttons, so she let him.

"What time is it now?" she asked.

"Twenty past."

"Well then, if I take a slow walk down the road, I shall just catch the half-past bus."

She was careful to say "I", but something, perhaps an over-emphasised avoidance of him, gave him the tip-off that he was invited too.

He picked up one of the bags from the floor, and opened the door for her.

Mrs Maxwell moved very slowly, as if she had to inch herself along as a solid block without moving her legs at all. Paul wasn't surprised with that coat on her, but found himself having to drag his feet, almost to walk backwards, in order to keep pace with her. After five minutes, they'd covered a distance Paul could have done in one, and he felt like biting off his fingers in frustration. The bus-stop was so close that Paul would not have left the house until the bus was due.

But on her feet, in the black coat, Mrs Maxwell looked more than ever like a teddy-bear, and teddy-bears weren't noted for being nimble; so Paul was patient.

There were several people at the stop when they reached it, a sure sign the bus would not be long, and it arrived soon after. When their turn came to get on, Paul went last, trying to help Mrs Maxwell up the steps from behind; but the conductor was more helpful, reaching down an arm, and saying, "Up you come, love." When Paul climbed up, he said to him, "Watch your granny don't tumble when we start, son."

Paul flopped down beside Mrs Maxwell and grinned at her. "He thinks you'm me gran."

"You must have told him, you monkey-pig," Mrs Maxwell said. "You keep your mouth shut in future and they'll take me for your auntie."

Now that *was* a joke. Paul was almost certain of it. But not certain enough to laugh, so he only grinned again, a little weakly.

After that they were silent for the rest of the ride. Paul couldn't think of anything to say that would interest such an old lady. She wouldn't know anything about his world. As for Mrs Maxwell, well, young people weren't interested in anything these days, and she didn't feel like talking. The shopping-trip exhausted her before it was begun.

At the bus-terminal Paul got off first, and Mrs Maxwell did him the honour of leaning on his shoulder as she came slowly down the bus steps. "Where first?" Paul asked, expecting a tour of the stores and at least two supermarkets.

"Where to *first*? The Co-op first, and then straight back home."

Paul laughed, and followed her as she slowly rolled along the street. He'd never been to the Co-op. "I've always gone there," the old lady said. "Must be fifty years. They look after you, the Co-op do. They give stamps."

"Green shield stamps?" Paul asked, walking backwards before her.

Mrs Maxwell gave him a look of stinging scorn. "Gree—no. They'm *blue*, Co-op stamps. They'm worth ten bob, a book of 'em."

"Oh," Paul said.

"Hey—hey—here we are. Where you going?"

Paul, walking backwards, and never having paid much attention to the Co-op, had passed it. He hurried back, and pushed open the door for her to pass through. He had to keep it open for several other women before he could rejoin Mrs Maxwell.

The Co-op wasn't impressive. A supermarket, it had only four tills, and only two of them were serving. The presentation wasn't as glossy as in other shops. The tins and jars seemed to be shoved on to the shelves any old way.

Mrs Maxwell was standing in the narrow aisle, undismayed

by the rush of shoppers, and the flash and slash of trolleys being returned to their rows, pondering over the baskets of tea.

"Which is the cheapest?" she asked Paul.

On some of the baskets were notices saying things like "Only 8p" with short dashes like a comic-book explosion drawn around the letters. With other brands, you had to hunt for the price. Paul triumphantly held up a packet of the Co-op's own. "Seven an' half!"

"That's the cheapest? Well, two quarters then."

Paul dropped the packets into the supermarket basket that hung over his arm, and followed her to a series of long shelves crammed with bread. "Large sliced," she said, and Paul put the basket on the floor while he used the lowest shelf as a step to help him get the bread from the top one.

The tinned vegetables, instant potato and dried beans on the other side of the aisle were ignored by the old lady, and the sauces and pickles, but at the cooked meats counter she bought a half-pound of bacon. Here she showed an unexpected side of her character.

First she inquired after the health, history and price of every slice of bacon on show, and found something wrong with each of them. That wasn't a good cut; that was too fat; that looked a funny colour; that didn't look fresh.

Paul listened with pride and amusement. He was sure that she had already decided what bacon she was going to have; there was the same obliqueness about her as when she had not asked Paul to go shopping with her. She was just out to cause a stir, that was all; as Paul often did himself. He did it to aggravate people, and to score off them, by making himself feel cleverer than they were. He supposed that Mrs Maxwell must feel the same vague need for revenge. He suspected that Mrs Maxwell, despite the great gaps between them of age and sex and attitudes, might have something of the same workings inside her head as he did.

She bought the bacon, finally, and Paul took the bag, with the price crayoned on it, from the irritated assistant, and followed Mrs Maxwell.

"I want some biscuits," she said.

Paul was surprised. Weren't old age pensioners supposed to be hard up? And weren't biscuits an expensive luxury? But the old lady instructed him to take three packets from the shelf, Milk Cookies, Shortcake and Digestive. Co-op biscuits, but still more than his mother would have spent on them, with three wages coming in.

"What about meat?" Paul asked. It seemed to him that the contents of the basket were on the starchy side.

Mrs Maxwell kept her back turned to the meat-fridge. "I can't afford meat."

"Yes you could," Paul said.

Mrs Maxwell stared stubbornly in front of her and wouldn't listen.

"It's good for you, meat," Paul argued. "Can't just live on biscuits."

"I got some bacon," the old lady said obstinately. "I got nowhere to keep it anyway."

Of course. Mrs Mentor had a fridge, and could buy two or three pieces of meat at a weekend and keep them until they were needed. Mrs Maxwell couldn't.

She had moved on to the dairy-fridge, snapping at a girl who was packing margarine further along the fridge, "What's the cheapest butter?"

"New Zealand," said the girl indifferently.

Paul checked, and the New Zealand was the cheapest. "A pound then," Mrs Maxwell said.

"You could get marge, that's cheaper," Paul said, but when he looked, he found that there wasn't much difference; in fact, some margarine was dearer than butter. "I always thought margarine was cheap," he said, personally injured. At the end of the fridge, Paul picked up a pound of the cheapest lard, and followed Mrs Maxwell as she made her slow but dogged way to the greengrocery counter. Here, waiting her turn, she studied everything on display. By the time her turn to be served came, she was, Paul was sure, certain of everything she was going to buy.

"How much am them sprouts?" she began.

The assistant, looking flushed and worried, snapped, "Six a pound."

"*Six?* They don't look much to me."

The assistant leaned on the counter and stared into space.

"They'm all spotty and grubby," Paul put in nervously, eager to join the game, but not certain that the two women would accept him. The assistant refocused on him with a distinctly hostile expression.

"What other greens have you got?" Mrs Maxwell asked.

The assistant intoned, "Spring cabbage, white cabbage, savoy; leeks, lettuce—that's all."

"How much is the Spring?"

"Eight a pound."

"Oh, that's too much," Mrs Maxwell said on a grumble.

"Looks all stringy to me," Paul said. "Lettuce pray it gets better." He couldn't keep a straight face, and both Mrs Maxwell and the assistant gave him stern looks.

"What about the leeks?" Mrs Maxwell asked, getting back to business.

"Twelve a pound."

"Mmm. Got a big un?"

The assistant turned one or two leeks over in a half-hearted way, and held one up for Mrs Maxwell's inspection.

"Have you got a bigger one?"

The assistant sighed heavily, and stooped to look again. Paul went to help her, energetically shifting leeks until, at the bottom of the pile, he found one as thick as a man's arm.

"How about this one, Mrs Maxwell?"

"Let me have a look." He took it to her, and she examined

all the leaves, weighed it in her hand. "I'll have that one."

As the assistant wrapped the leek, Mrs Maxwell launched another attack. "What am the 'taters?"

"Three a pound." Paul looked up quickly at the assistant's voice. It sounded as if she was speaking through gritted teeth.

"Oh," Mrs Maxwell said. "Well, I'd take five pound to save me coming out again, but I couldn't carry them." Thoughtful pause. "I could take two pounds, but it's all carriage." Another pause. "I'd better leave it."

The assistant rolled her eyes upwards. Paul said, "I'm here. I'll carry 'em."

Mrs Maxwell retaliated by looking the other way and pretending not to hear.

"So what?" the assistant demanded. "Do you want the 'taters, or don't you?"

Paul continued to look at Mrs Maxwell, waiting for some sign. But she avoided his eye.

"Well?" asked the assistant.

"Five pound please," Paul said.

"And I'll have half-pound of them sprouts," Mrs Maxwell said.

"Certainly." The assistant's voice sounded sarcastic.

With the potatoes under one arm, Paul left the counter in the wake of Mrs Maxwell. Weighted with the basket, he found it easier to keep pace with her, but she still moved very slowly. She rolled, with complete indifference, past the tinned meats, and bottles of pop, and cereals, and washing-powders, but put seven bags of crisps into the basket. Then they had to stand in a queue.

Paul grew bored. He shifted his weight from foot to foot, and the weight of the basket from arm to arm. For a minute or so he tried to hum with the taped music, but it was so soapy that it slipped from his mind. He began to peer into other people's shopping baskets. The woman in front had a round 'air-freshener' which you opened up a little more each day to let the smell out, and six cans of dog food, costing fourteen pence each. The woman behind had two bags of coloured cotton-wool balls, and a packet of plastic bags for roasting meat in.

"I spy with my little eye, something beginning with 'M'," he said loudly to Mrs Maxwell.

"What's that, my love?"

"Mugs," Paul said.

The woman behind carefully ignored him.

Mrs Maxwell sniggered.

Encouraged, Paul asked, "Don't you want any paper towels for your kitchen—or instant puddin'—just add milk, eggs, fruit and anything else you can think of?"

"All I can do to live, let alone buy stuff like that," Mrs Maxwell said seriously, damping Paul's humour just when he thought he had a routine going.

When they reached the till the girl was slamming shut the drawer. Staring off in the other direction, she tapped a notice taped to the side of her machine, which said, "All coupons, stamp-books, empty bottles, etc., *must* be handed in before the goods are rung up." "Any coupons?"

Mrs Maxwell looked confused. The girl turned her head, looked straight through the old lady and snapped, "Any coupons?"

"Ah—no," Paul said, and heaved the basket up beside the till, dumping the potatoes on top.

The girl threw the things out of the basket and on to the belt, her fingers leaping over the key-board. Then she rammed the belt over and shunted everything down into one of the bays behind her. Triumphantly she thumped the black button and rang up the total.

"One pound seventy, please."

Mrs Maxwell began to feel in various pockets, while the cashier beat her green finger-nails on her till. After three or four minutes Mrs Maxwell found her purse and brought it out with stiff fingers. She began to fumble at the clasp, and the cashier sighed.

"Here," Paul said. He came around the till, took the purse, opened it and gave the girl a five-pound note.

"Hey," Mrs Maxwell said, "hey you. That's my money. Hey—you watch it, you——"

"It's all right, it's all right," Paul said.

The girl counted the change into his hand, and, as he turned away, said, "Stamps!" She pushed some folded Co-op stamps at him.

"Thanks a million," Paul said.

"Don't you lose 'em, don't you lose them stamps," Mrs Maxwell said. She was trying to put the tea into the bag without moving her fingers.

"That's why I'm here," Paul said, annoyed, and took the bag from her. "The stamps am all right. They'm in your purse. Here it is." He dropped it into her pocket.

"Did her give you the right money?"

"Yes, she did."

Mrs Maxwell stood and watched him pack the bag. She waited until he had finished, then took the purse from her pocket again, and gave it to him. "I want a four of Guinness."

Paul grinned and put the bag down at her feet, went to fetch the booze from the wine-counter. Coming back he said, "Am we set now? Where next?"

"Where to next, is it? It's all right for you, ain't it, where to next. I ain't as light on me feet as you am, my lad. Home, that's where next."

"Home," Paul said. He'd thought she'd been joking when she'd said they were only going to Co-op. It wasn't worth coming all the way to town just to visit the Co-op.

"Are you coming?" Mrs Maxwell asked. "Or have I got to carry the bag meself now?"

Well, whatever turns you on, Paul thought, and said, "All right then. Come on."

When they reached the bus-stop, they'd missed their bus. Luckily the bus-terminal was built around an island with grass in the middle, and they were able to sit on the wall built around the lawn.

Paul grew bored and left the bag with Mrs Maxwell while he went over to the time-table and tried to decipher it. Pushing back through the Saturday bus-queues, he said, "We've just missed the 120, but we can catch the D7 in a minute, it goes the same way."

"Yes, but then I shall have to walk from the 'Jug'."

Paul opened his mouth to say that it was only a few yards further from the 'Jug of Punch' stop, and that they'd have to wait another hour for the next 120—but turned his head instead and looked intently at her face: that calm face with its folds and folds of brown skin, the spectacles on the end of the short nose; the set, determined look.

That was old; not being able to walk fifty yards more.

And not minding waiting an hour.

He wouldn't have waited for any bus, he couldn't stand hanging about. He would have walked. It wouldn't have taken him half an hour.

He thought: Seventy years. She's lived for seventy years, or maybe even longer.

He gazed at her in awe. He wasn't sixteen yet. Two sixteens were thirty-two; four were sixty-four; five were— eighty. So four times. Four times as long as him. She'd been elderly when he'd been born. She'd had kids and grand-kids. . . .

1905 when she'd been born. Before the First World War. She'd lived through *both* wars. She'd been a full-grown woman, probably married when the Second World War had broken out, when his own parents had just been children. And he'd been thinking her helpless, and stupid; treating *her* like a child.

She'd forgotten more than he'd learned yet.

Paul felt very small.

He also felt very cold by the time they'd waited an hour and a quarter for the 120. This time he remembered, and got on the bus first to help Mrs Maxwell up the steps. He managed to find her a seat, but he had to stand, rocking and jerking as the bus made its way through the traffic.

Mrs Maxwell was tired. When they got off the bus, she made even heavier weather than before of the walk up the hill. Paul couldn't understand it. She'd been sitting down on the wall, and on the bus, but here she was, wheezing and blowing, and having to stop for rests. It worried him. He kept chivvying round her, asking her to stop again, get her breath back; peering anxiously into her face for signs of glaze in her eyes. He was afraid that she might have a heart attack, or a stroke or something.

It was with great relief that he reached the house door. He took the purse from the bag and found the key, and opened up. "Sit down," he said. "C'mon, you sit in your chair and I'll make you a cup of tea."

"Wait a minute, wait a minute. Let me get me coat off." She was pulling at the thick buttons. Paul dropped the shopping bag on his way to the kitchen and came back to unbutton it for her. He helped her out of it, and draped the shawl from the back of her chair around her instead. When she was comfortable in her chair, he took her coat and the bags into the kitchen, and put the kettle on. Then he came back and made the fire up again. Kneeling on the hearth with the poker and the box of coal, he said, "Next time, I'll get the shoppin' in on me own."

The old lady sniggered. "Every other week I go shoppin', and bring the bag back on me own. It ain't killed me yet." And when Paul quickly looked up, she said, "I shall die when I'm ready, and not before."

Paul coughed. "Ah, yes," he said, and went out to empty the teapot in the yard. Mrs Maxwell smiled at the fire.

Paul made the tea in the kitchen and took two cups into the

living-room. He gave one to Mrs Maxwell, and sat down on a footstool before the fire with his own.

The old lady took a sip of the hot tea and became talkative. "What did you say your name was?"

"Paul Mentor," Paul said, wondering if it was worth it all.

"Where d'you live, Paul?"

"Oh—over the hill. Wurnley. You know. The housing estate."

"Oh yes," said the old lady. "I know." But she didn't know at all. "You catch the bus?"

"No," Paul said. "I walked. It isn't far."

The old lady laughed. "I could have said that once. You got brothers and sisters?"

"I got one sister. She's older than me. She's twenty-two."

"Only one sister?"

"Yeah. There's just me and her. And me Mom and Dad." Paul spoke without enthusiasm. He contrasted this close, gloomy little house, its ticking clock and spitting coal-fire, the hot cup of tea between his hands, with his own home, the television blaring, the bare walls, the air of being unfinished, a camping-place. He wanted to sit close to the fire on the little stool and never move.

But he supposed he would have to go home.

"I could come again in the morning," he said. "Make the fire, wash up."

"If you like," she said.

He drank his tea and washed the leaves about, trying to see pictures in them, and sat for a long time with the cup growing cool in his hands. Above his head the clock ticked, and he knew he would have to go sooner or later. Anyway, he had nothing to stay for.

"Can you manage now?" he asked.

"I did last night and every night before," she said.

He stood up and took her cup, washed them in the kitchen, dried them and stood them in line on the dresser. He wandered back into the living-room. "I'll be off then."

"If you like," the old lady said.

"Sure you can manage?"

"I'm sure," she said, smiling at the fire.

Paul picked up his jacket and edged towards the door. The house seemed suddenly very dark and very silent. He didn't like leaving her alone in it. He didn't like shutting the door, and closing her in.

He went back and switched on her radio. The light-switch was by the door, and he pushed it down before leaving. "Ta-ra then."

"Ta-ra, love. Watch how you go. It has been nice having somebody round."

"Oh! That's—that's all right. Been nice coming. Well—ta-ra."

"Ta-ra."

"I'll come tomorrow."

"If you like."

Paul sighed, slipped out, and shut the door quickly behind him. Outside it was already growing dusk. He stood for a moment with his hand clenched on the knob, fighting a rising panic which said that shutting the door had ended her for him, and him for her. He wanted to open the door again and look in, to see that she was still there. But that was stupid. Of course she was.

He let go of the knob and began the walk home. But it felt as if part of his gut was missing, left behind.

Mrs Maxwell hauled herself from her chair and moved slowly across the room, to switch off the light so that she could sit in the dark.

It was full dark when Paul reached home. He took the key from around his neck and went in. Only his sister Kath was home, in a long skirt today, drawing round her mouth with lipstick. She looked over her shoulder when he came in.

"Your dinner's on a saucepan," she said.

Paul picked up a pair of tights, a pair of knickers and a blouse from the settee, threw them into his mother's chair, and sat down. "Where's Mom and Dad?"

"Mom got him to take her to the pictures. Oh—get the door. That'll be Babs."

Paul got up and dragged down the hall, where he let in Babs, Kath's girl-friend. In she came, foggy with perfume, her eyes all black and green and shiny, a black maxi coat and a little tight hat. "Hel*lo*, Paul. How are you, kid?"

"Supercalafragilistic," Paul said, dead-pan, and she tittered.

Kath called from the living-room to come on in, and Babs did, with Paul following.

"Shan't be a sec, Babs, I'm nearly ready, just got to get me coat, sit down," Kath said, and dashed out of the room. As her footsteps clumped up the stairs, Paul said, "Sure. Pull up an ironing-board and sit down."

The ironing-board and the clothes-horse were still there, although the washing-basket had been moved to his father's chair. Babs stood behind the settee and simpered. "Just like our house," she said, untruthfully.

Then Kath came down again, pulling on her coat. She stuck her head into the living-room, to say, "Oh Paul—Mom said to tell you her'd left fifty pence on the shelf for you to get you some cider or sweets or summat. Ta-ra." Babs went out with her, and the door slammed. The house fell silent.

Paul found the money and put it in his pocket before fetching his dinner from the kitchen, bringing it in with a towel under the hot plate. He put it on the table while he took the washing-basket from his father's chair and threw it over the back of the settee. It bounced once or twice and lay still.

He switched on the television, and adjusted the chair for better viewing. He climbed into it and was enveloped. The chair was just too big for him. His dinner was on the end of the table, and he leaned across to eat it with a fork taken from an empty plate.

And when Kojak had got his man, but his parents hadn't come home, he switched the television off and went to bed.

Chapter Four

"Paul, I'm off now. Switch the lights off, and the fire off——"

"And lock the back door; I know," Paul said.

"And lock the back door. Have you got your dinner-money?"

"Yais Mater."

"You what?"

"Yes, I have."

"Do you need any more? In case you need anythin'?"

"No," Paul said patiently.

"Well, don't forget to fetch that milk. We'll have no tea tonight else."

"I'll remember."

"All right, look after yourself. Be careful on them roads." The door slammed behind her. The house retreated into silence.

Then the gas-fire began to hiss, and a chair creaked.

Paul put his cup down on the coffee-table, and fetched his school shirt from the clothes-horse. It felt cool and stiff as he slipped it on. Eight o'clock.

He poured himself another cup of tea and threw the washing-basket off the settee so that he could lie full-length among the cushions, towels, newspapers, old vests, stockings, a one-armed gorilla on a long elastic band, a fur coat, three pop bottles and a pair of suede shoes.

He put the cup on the floor and dangled the gorilla over the side of the settee, making it leap up and down on its elastic. At half-past eight he swung it around and around until it blurred into a circle, and then let it go. It flew up and hit the wall near the ceiling, rebounded with force, and hit the blue vase on the mantelpiece. Even as Paul rolled from the settee in a shower of socks and knickers, the vase fell from the shelf, and cracked open on the tiled surround.

In times of crisis, Paul thought fast. Almost jumping the table, he came to a crouch over the broken pieces, picking them up and fitting them together. Two lodged well, but a piece was missing from one side, and he hadn't time to fix it.

He thought of wedging the pieces together and balancing them in place on the shelf. It might be a fortnight before the vase was discovered to be broken, and then they couldn't say he'd done it. But then he had a better idea. He fetched the sea-shell-covered bottle from the sideboard, and put it on the shelf where the vase had been. Then he carefully picked up all the pieces of the broken vase, and carried them out into the front room, where he slipped them into the pocket of his jacket. He put the jacket on, and had the front door open before he remembered the gas-fire, and the light, and the back door. He hurried back to switch off and lock up. Twenty-five to nine. After. He was going to be late. Oh well. He'd been late before.

Slamming the door behind him, he started on his way to school. At the first piece of waste ground he stopped to empty the pieces of vase from his pocket, and scatter them amongst the long grass.

Turning a corner, he saw ahead of him Mike, Tony and Mal. They were late too, but not as late as he was. He ran, coming down on them before they recognized the footsteps and turned. He jumped and slapped his hands down on Mal's and Mike's shoulders, propelling himself up, above their heads, and forward to land in front of them.

"Paul!" Mike said, as he recovered his balance.

"Might have bloody known," Mal said, brushing at his jacket.

"Mentor, where have you been?" Mike demanded. "Was up your house twice yesterday, and you weren't in."

"Ooh," Paul said. "I was going along, mindin' me own business Friday night, and this great big blonde grabbed me and dragged me into her house against me will, and we was there all the weekend—having *sex*," he said with a wink, and a leer, and a stagger suggestive of Quasimodo.

Mal and Tony went into their sophisticated routine. "Isn't he *crude*?" Mal asked.

"A grubby, spotty, evil-minded little Herbert," Tony said.

"His mother and father struggling to bring him up Godly."

"And he's so *crude*," Tony said.

Mike said, "Did you go and see that old lady?"

"Old lady?" Paul said, with instant blankness. "What old lady?"

"You know. The one Archer took us to see."

"Oh, that one," Paul said. "I din't! Think I'm saft or summat?"

"Where've you been then, eh?"

Paul looked at his watch. "We'm goin' to be late—come on!" He ran down the road, calling, "Hurry up!" as if it was the worst thing in the world, to be late. Mike and Tony and Mal glanced at each other in surprise, and sauntered on after him.

They went into the school grounds by a side gate, and followed the path until it made a bend, then cut across the playing-field, which was strictly forbidden, but so what? Through the windows of the school they could see the classrooms emptying, and the corridors full of jostling, pushing pupils.

"Bell's gone for Assembly," Mike said.

Near the side door they would have entered by was a wooden shed, used for the storage of sports-gear. Now the door slowly opened, and Paul's head came out. "Oi—in here."

As one man, Tony, Mike and Mal swung over to the shed and ducked inside.

"Safe as houses in here," Paul said. "Better than the bogs." He was crouched on top of a pile of gym-mats, like a gnome on a toadstool. Tony punched him in the shoulder. "Trust a cunning little tool like thee to think of a place like this."

"What if somebody saw us come in?" Mike asked.

Tony shouted him down. "*Nobody* saw us come in, dope."

Mal produced a packet of cigarettes, casually showing off again. "Here, Tone—fake?" Tony took one, and found a match in his pocket, pretended to strike it on Paul's head. Mal offered the cigarettes to Mike.

"No thanks," Mike said. "I don't smoke."

Mal pushed the packet at Paul instead, saying, "Dope."

Paul struck upwards at the packet with the back of his hand, sending the packet and all the cigarettes flying. "You'm the dope for smokin'."

Mal gave an agonized squeal, and fell on his hands and knees to search amongst the bats and wire and shuttlecocks for his cigarettes. "What you want to do that for?" he asked indignantly as he raised the dust. And, as Paul rocked with laughter on his throne of gym-mats, "If I can't find 'em all, I'll duff you up, Mentor."

"Ooo—*butch*," Paul said, flapping one hand, and Tony and Mike joined him in laughing at Mal.

Mal knelt up in the centre of the floor, counting the cigarettes he had found. "Lucky for you, Mentor——"

"Oh, I'm saved," Paul said.

"I'd have smashed you in."

"Aah," Paul said.

Mal pointed a threatening finger, and said, "You'm askin' for it, Mentor. I'll give thee a one-er in a minute."

"Aah, go on then," Paul said, pushing his face forward, daring him. He knew that even if Mal did hit him, Mal would be the loser, since he was so much bigger than Paul.

"Knock it off," Mike said nervously. Mike disliked any kind of disturbance.

"Knock it off? He nearly lost me my fakes!" Mal waved the packet under Mike's nose. "They cost money, you know."

Mike tried to laugh it off. "You don't want 'em. They'll stunt your growth."

"Huh," Mal said. "Is that why he don't smoke then? If his growth was stunted, he'd disappear."

Paul launched himself from the mats, to crash head-first into Mal's stomach. He knocked Mal back against the wall, bringing down a net full of tennis balls. But although he clenched his fists in Mal's jersey, and used his head like a battering ram, he wasn't strong enough to do much damage, and certainly not strong enough to protect himself from a counter-attack.

Mal stooped and punched him in the stomach. Paul gasped as the air was driven out of him, and Mal pushed him over, going down on top of him, and punching again.

"Hey!" Mike shouted, and jumped up from the form he was sitting on. Tony straightened from the wall where he'd been leaning, and pulled at Mal's arm. Mike took a handful of his hair, and together they hauled him up.

Paul rolled to a sitting position, breathless and bristling.

"You all right?" Mike asked.

"'Course I'm all right!" Paul cried, glaring at Mal. "He couldn't knock a fly off a rice-puddin', he couldn't!"

Mal sneered as he pulled his jersey and jacket straight. Like Paul, he was a little short of breath. "Well, that'll teach *you*, Mentor," he said, but he turned away from the others.

Mike looked at his watch. He was a past master at changing the subject. "Twenty-five to ten. Assembly should be over."

Tony cautiously stuck his head out. "Yeah. They'm comin' back." He paused. "Who's going to put the marks in the register?" This was a lone mission, entailing some risk. Their eyes shifted away from each other's eyes.

But Paul, well below the clash of meaningful looks, piped up, "I'll go."

"All right then," Tony said happily, and they prepared to abandon the shed. They slipped out and ran across the piece of grass, and in through the door to join the lines and jumble of kids coming back from Assembly.

"I'll take your books to first lesson," Mike shouted to Paul, and then Paul disappeared in the crush, fighting gamely against the stream.

Paul made his way along the corridor, walking in the clear space between the lines of pupils when he could. But where there were no patrolling prefects or teachers, the corridor became a mass of pushing, shoving bodies and Paul had to fight or slip through as best he could.

Eventually he reached the foyer at the main entrance of the school, where the tables were being set out for the school dinners. Opening off the foyer were the school's impressive assembly hall, and the administration corridor. Paul turned into this corridor, keeping an eye peeled for trouble. The administration corridor was full of trouble. There was the Headmaster's office, the Headmistress's office, the Deputy Head's office, and the school secretary's office. The secretary was worse than any of the Heads. It was to the cupboard outside the secretary's office that the registers were delivered by the monitors from each class.

There were seven classes in each form and, because it was a Comprehensive School, they had been named C, O, M, P, R, E and H. They were summed up by pupils and staff thus: C, O and M were the top or grammar streams; P and R the intermediate or secondary. E was for 'backward' or technical education and H for the mentally subnormal, or H for Horrendous. The pupils of the school weren't supposed to know this, and the letters denoting classes were changed every now and then, but it didn't make any difference.

Paul, Tony and Mike were all members of 5O, while Mal

was in 5C. Mal had a tendency to rub this in, but it didn't mean anything really. O was an overflow class, and wasn't included in every year. C and O followed the same syllabus, but if you were weak on languages you were put into O, which only taught French, while in C you took French and German. Similarly, if you wanted to take C.S.E. or "O" levels in a certain subject, you were promoted from M to O to try for them. Not many people below C and O took the examinations.

Paul sat down on one of the chairs near the cupboard, in order to disguise himself as someone with a right to be there. Those who had come to be punished always stood. He took the registers on to his lap and sorted through them until he found 5C and 5O. One of the little gang waiting outside the Head's office said, "Late again, Mentor."

Paul didn't answer. With a black pen from his pocket, he marked himself, Tony and Mike present for that morning and afternoon. Then he put 5O's register back in the middle of the pile.

He opened 5C's register and found Mal's name. He put the black pen back in his pocket and took out a red one. Instead of a slanting line across the little square, he drew in a red nought. And for the afternoon. And for several weeks after. That should raise the pigeons, and they would all come home to Mal.

So he took his petty revenge, slapped the register on the top of the pile, and ran to his first class.

The first and second lessons were Biology, held not in the New! Improved! Science Block, with all mod cons, but in the school's old science wing, which was like something out of *Tom Brown*. The long, drab corridor was lined on both sides with lockers, covered with inky messages, and you found your way to the rooms by smell. Gas and burnt rubber and oil was the Physics room; a wave of ammonia and sulphur announced the Chemistry lab; and, finally, the thin, forbidding scent of formaldehyde crawled from the Biology room. In he went.

Mr Hayes was leaning on the desk, his grey hair in turmoil, grilling the rest of 5O about their homework. "Ah," he said, turning as the door opened. "Mentor," he said, with sadistic pleasure. "And where have you been, my little lotus-flower?"

"I had to go over to the new block and feed Miss Allsop's piranha fish, sir."

Mr Hayes watched him with a frozen grin for a minute or two, then said, "Very good, Mentor. I want you to read very carefully what I have written across your homework. Now go to your place and behave."

The old science rooms had long, high tables, with high wooden stools to sit on. The first two tables were occupied by the girls, whom Paul passed without a glance—or without a direct glance anyway. Behind, at the third table, were the boys. Paul climbed on to his stool by the staves and hunched over the books which Mike had put at his place. "I put in the marks," he whispered to Mike.

A girl came round, throwing their books to them, and Paul opened his to find, written all across his half-page of homework, "You can do much better than this tripe. You are not trying. Do it again for next week, besides next week's homework." "Oh, sod," Paul said, and gave the teacher a secretive two-fingers sign.

The lesson was about soil-humus and worms, with the promise of some "experiments" in the lesson next week. "Oh thrill," Paul whispered. But Mr Hayes had a strong personality and Paul did not raise his voice. Besides, he was a good teacher, and amusing to listen to. He had no trouble with a class of 5O's calibre, and time was passed, profitably as they say, until a quarter to eleven and break.

At break Paul asked Mike to take his books back to his locker and himself ran over to the coal-bunker behind the kitchens. This was where one of the games of Toss-penny was being held, until it was discovered, and the players hauled before the Headmaster. After that it would be moved somewhere else. Gambling with pennies and cards, like running in the corridors, walking on the grass, talking in Assembly, skipping Assembly, coming to school on a bike and carrying your briefcase in your right hand, was strictly forbidden, but, like all the other forbidden things, gambling thrived. Paul was a regular player of Toss-penny, and was lucky. He always got out while he was ahead, and had never yet lost his dinner-money. On this break, he won eight and a half pence, and collected his books for the English lesson well pleased.

Mr Gillian, the English teacher, was not a Mr Hayes. He was an intelligent, gentle man, with a great love of his subject and a delicate wit. He was just too sensitive to be a teacher.

They were reading, in the Monday lesson, a book Mr Gillian had got from the stores. He had them reading parts of it aloud around the class, interrupting them only for long, boring asides on "style" or lack of it, and "allusion", and the "hallmark of true literature".

The book was a swashbuckling tale of the age of sail—so the blurb said—and Paul privately thought it was meant for younger classes. Possibly old Gillian had them confused with 2O.

A further burden was that Paul, through having had more practice, could read faster and more fluently than most others in his class. Even though they were 5O and not 5E, Paul considered most of them to be almost illiterate. There was Williams, who blundered over every word with more than four letters (he knew most words with four letters) and Hammond, who ignored all punctuation, and—but all of them read very, very slowly, reducing all the story to a drone.

Paul quickly became bored, and began to read ahead of the class in the book he shared with Mike. The more he read of it, the less he liked it. It reminded him of Errol Flynn, and that kind of ancient film. So his mind strayed to other things, and when he came across the word "rapier", he began to snigger.

"What's up?" Mike asked.

"Rapier," Paul said. Mike, his head almost on the book, stared at him.

Paul pointed to the girls' bottoms, wriggling about on their chairs in front. "Rap-ier," he said. Mike frowned in puzzlement, then half-laughed. "What're you on about?"

"Rap-ier—rape 'yer," Paul hissed, annoyed at having to spell it out, but then giggled again.

"Oh dear, oh dear," Mike said, very superior, but then collapsed in red-faced snickers all over the book.

"Rap-ier, rap-ier, rap-ier!" Paul said, on a rising note, but then his third "ier" came out a bit too loud, coinciding with the present reader faltering into silence. The class turned. Mr Gillian craned his neck to see them.

"Ah—er—Mentor. Have you—ah—something of—ah—importance—to—ah—impart to us?"

"No sir, I don't think so," Paul said cheerfully, and won the class to his side immediately.

"Then what were you—ah—singing—just then?"

" 'Rapier', sir."

" 'Rapier'?"

"Yessir, 'rapier'."

The class began to laugh, and Mr Gillian couldn't stop them. Mike beside Paul, had his hand over all his face to hide it from the teacher, and was making strange bubbling sounds. "Ah—why 'rapier', Mentor?"

"Why not, sir?"

Mr Gillian wisely gave up a struggle he was not equal to. "Ah—why not indeed, Mentor? I think you had better read the next few paragraphs."

Mike flipped the pages back, and pointed out where the class had reached. Paul began to read. He read smoothly, and without stammering or mispronunciation, observed all the punctuation marks and, above all, did not drone. He pulled the rug from beneath Mr. Gillian's feet.

"Ah—er—very good, Mentor. It might be even better if you paid more attention, hmm?"

"No sir." The class hummed again.

"I beg your pardon, Mentor?"

"Yessir."

Mr Gillian then gave him a very straight look which was supposed to be intimidating. Smiling, Paul stared him out, but he was sad when the lesson resumed. Mr Gillian was a sad man, timid, unprotected, and Paul pitied him.

Then it was dinner-time. Paul accompanied Mike out to the yard where, seated on the wide windowsills, he watched him eat his sandwiches.

"Want one?" Mike asked, and Paul shook his head. Paul stayed to school-dinners, and would be going soon, at ten to one. He pulled a lump of bread from one of Mike's sandwiches, and threw it to a sparrow.

"Hey! My Mom didn't pack these to feed spugs, you know."

"Belt up," Paul said.

When he'd finished his sandwiches, Mike wanted to take a stroll around the school to see what was going on, so Paul left him, going instead to the doors where the queue formed for second dinner. Already second diners were hanging about, determined to get a good place in the queue. One of them was Mal, whom Paul avoided, sliding off to one side and leaning against the wall.

At a quarter to one the queue began to line up, and Paul went to join it. He would have been tenth, something like that, but a voice called to him, "Paul—hey, Paul—up here!" It was Mal, who had managed to get second in the line. Paul hesitated, and then realized that Mal would not be accused of sabotaging the register until roll-call that afternoon. Paul smiled, as Judas must have done, and went up the line.

"Hey—that ain't fair!" said the holder of the third place. He was a big 4H boy. Not much ever penetrated his skull, but the fact that Paul was bodging the queue did. "Get to the back, thee."

"I'm getting in here," Paul said, neatly slipping in front of Mal.

"He's bodged the queue!" cried the 4H boy, raising the battle-cry for all the other E's and H's, who were always incensed by such infringements of their rights as queuebodging.

Mal turned round and looked down his long, thin nose at him. "Hard luck," he said, then turned his back and leaned over to the girls' line opposite. "Hey—Diane—save us a place, and I'll sit by you."

"Can't," Diane said. "Mrs Paget won't let me."

"Aah—go on. Try."

"Can't," Diane said.

Paul was relieved. It wasn't that he didn't like Diane. The trouble was, he did. He knew that if they sat with her, at a girls' table, he would either be uncomfortably silent and drop his cutlery, or would gabble on and on until even he thought himself an idiot. And if Mal sat with her on his own, then he would be jealous.

It wasn't fair. How could you chat easily with a girl when you couldn't see her face for the bulge of her blouse? And how could you ask a girl out when she towered over you, and she'd look like big sister taking little brother on a treat?

Mrs Paget, the "dinner-lady", appeared. She was short, but not so short as Paul, and he ground his teeth. Her build was also impressive, she had a bow-wave. Her hair was piled up on her head and dyed a harsh red, and her face was powdered until it was orange.

"Gels—walk in, please," she said, and the girls' queue began to troop into the building.

"Gels—walk in, plaise," Paul called out, and Mal shoved him from behind. If Mrs Paget was annoyed, they would be made to queue longer. "What you doin'?" Paul demanded indignantly. He didn't even know that he had mimicked Mrs Paget; he did it without thinking.

Mrs Paget counted in twenty girls, and then stopped them. A teacher on dinner duty would sometimes send in twenty boys next, but not Mrs Paget. After a few minutes she called again, "Walk in gels."

"What about Women's Lib?" Paul asked sourly, and Mal shoved him again. But Mrs Paget had a soft spot for Paul, taken in by his choir-boy looks every bit as much as old ladies were. She strutted along to them, arriving well in front of herself, and said, "You should *always* let the gels go first. You want to be a gentleman, don't you?"

"No," Paul said. "I want me dinner."

Mrs Paget laughed indulgently and waggled back to the steps, calling, "Gels, please."

"Old Cow," Paul said.

"You'm all right, you ungrateful little so and so," Mal said. "She's always nice enough to you. She never reports you."

"Old cow," Paul said.

But the next troop of girls was four short of twenty, so Mal, Paul—and the 4H boy got in. They raced down the corridor and across the foyer—where Diane hadn't been able to save places—and began to queue outside the kitchens.

Just inside the kitchen sat a prefect with a wooden box, to collect the dinner-money, twelve and a half pence, and you had to have the right change or go to the back. Mal had only two ten-pence pieces, and tried to arrange with Paul that Paul would pay for both of them, and Mal would owe him. But Paul thought that after Mal's register was opened, he probably wouldn't get his money; so Mal had to make the deal with the boy in front. The 4H boy was looking back down the corridor for the first sight of his friends, and guffawing because he had got in before them.

They went in, paying their money, and jostled up to the

serving-hatches, taking plates from the stacks. There was steak-and-kidney pie, or heart, or thin slices of pork, in big silver trays.

"Steak and kidley please," Paul said, shoving out his plate. The cook smiled and scraped a portion on to his plate.

"You ought to have heart, like me," Mal was saying. "It's really nice. You'd really like it." But he was only showing off again, and Paul ignored him.

They moved on, in a din of metal trays and crockery, to the next hatch, where there was spinach, or carrots, or cabbage. Paul had cabbage and begged for some carrots too—and got them. That was one advantage of being small, not to mention looking like a choir-boy; the cooks felt that they should feed you up.

Then two scoops of potatoes each, and dodging out again before the cook on the end could pour gravy over your dinner. The dinners were very good, but the gravy was to be avoided at all costs. It was grey slime. That last cook's job was a thankless one.

"Gravy?" she would ask, her jug poised, a hopeless smile stuck lopsidedly to her face.

"Yerg! No—spare me!" Paul said, and shot past.

And, "No thank *you*!" Mal said, and even the 4H thug knew enough to refuse it.

Outside, in the foyer, there was a great clamour of voices, and knives and forks, and crockery. The other dinner-lady, Mrs Sergeant, herded them with screams and yells to a table at the far end, just vacated by the first diners. Paul slammed his plate down in a pool of water, and sat in, while around him others arrived with clattering plates and scraping chairs. There wasn't much scintillating conversation, because the last one to finish had, by custom, to take the water-jug and cups from the table, and that meant wasted minutes from the dinner-hour. Therefore they all ate with speed and desperation. Paul ate all of the pie and about half of the rest of what he had on his plate, then dusted it brown with pepper, white with salt, mashed it all up, emptied his tin cup of water into it, stirred it about, and then took his plate and cutlery over to where the pudding trolley had been set up. There was a bowl for the waste, a bowl for the cutlery, and a bowl for the plates. Then snatch up a pudding-dish, and look over the puddings. Bakewell tart, or sago with jam, or ice-cream with hot chocolate sauce. Paul took the ice-cream, and squeezed back between the tables, resisting the impulse to pour the hot sauce down somebody's neck. Again he ate about half of it and then began to feel full. So he melted the remaining ice-cream in the sauce and, pausing only to salt the drinking water so that the others couldn't have another drink, took his dish to the bowls set out for the pudding-dishes. He sauntered outside to look for Mike.

The lesson after dinner was Maths, at which Mike was good, but Paul was terrible. The simple addition, subtraction, multiplication and division he could manage, given enough time and paper, but anything beyond that baffled him. He couldn't see any use, even, in dropping lines through triangles and putting tangents on circles. What did it prove? And supposing you could prove it, what the hell did it matter? When he got tired of floundering in the darkness, he would go to the teacher to ask for advice, and then engage him in long, wandering conversations, about the teacher's new car, or the French teacher's beard, or the men who had come to mow the lawns, or the latest film at the local flicks, or any other subject which made itself available, until the teacher realized what was happening and insisted on teaching Maths.

At the end of the lesson they streamed from the classroom into the hotch-potch of the corridor, on their way to the cloak-room where they had their history lesson on a Monday, because all other classrooms were taken. The corridor was choked with people, and they were shuffling along when suddenly, in the flood coming the other way, Paul saw Mal's face. A second, and Mal saw him too. His face lit up with malice, and he raised a clenched fist. Paul knew the form—a swift punch to the head as they passed. There were no prefects or teachers about to prevent it.

Paul wriggled behind Mike, between Mike and the wall, clinging to his blazer and dodging about as Mal tried to reach him. Mike laughed and protested, but between the two of them he could do nothing but stagger from side to side. Then a great voice roared out, "Malcolm Mathews! You're blocking the corridor!"

"I'll get you, Mentor," Mal hissed, and was taken away by the crowd.

"What you done to *him*?" Mike asked, as Paul emerged from beneath his arm.

"Nothin'," Paul said blithely. "He must be barmy."

"Oh ar," Mike said. "But I know you."

It is difficult to hold a lesson in a cloakroom, but the teacher did his best. An earnest young man, he looked like the actors who are always chosen to play earnest young curates. He had the square glasses, and the trick of pushing his lips forward when he spoke. He managed to cram them, girls and boys, into four cloakrooms, and went from group to group. The lesson was supposed to be on the reformation of working conditions in the nineteenth century. For a while it was. But as the teacher paused for breath between the first and second Factory Acts, Paul said, "Mr Ward, sir, I been wondering——"

Mr Ward sighed. He knew this ploy of old. He also knew that ignoring it would serve no purpose. "*What* have you been wondering, Mentor?"

"How many wives did Henry VIII have?"

A slow grin spread over Mr Ward's face. "Now, Mentor," he said, "you know very well how many wives Henry VIII had."

"No, I don't, honestly, sir."

Mr Ward smiled again. "The second Factory Act——"

"But my Mom said he had eight wives and they all had their heads chopped off."

"*Mentor*," Mr Ward said, and the cloakroom filled with laughter. People peered around from other cloakrooms to see what was happening.

"What, sir?" Paul asked, his brown eyes stretched to their widest, his mouth an "O".

"Be quiet—and listen."

"But I want to put her right, sir. I don't like her to be wrong about a thing like that. She *is* wrong, isn't she, sir?"

Mr Ward rubbed at his hair, and surrendered. "If I tell you, will you be quiet?—Henry VIII had six wives, and only two were executed. One he divorced, one died in—er—childbirth, one he never properly married at all, and one outlived him. *Now*, the second Factory Act——"

But as he began for the third time on the second Factory Act, Paul continued to stare at him with such intensity that he asked nervously, "What is it now, Mentor?"

"Why did you go all red when you said 'childbirth', sir?"

Mr Ward stretched both hands out towards his throat. "How you've survived this long——"

But, by then, there was such an uproar from the furthest cloakrooms that he had to leave them in order to maintain order. In fact, most of the lesson was spent on orders to be quiet, because when the far cloakrooms were quiet, those in the centre were Bedlam, and vice versa.

At four o'clock, they went back to their form-rooms to be dismissed. Mike had got together some books, but Paul had decided that all his homework could wait—probably until it had to be handed in. Just as they were about to leave, Mr Archer stooped into the room, tall, angular and Christian. He nodded to the form-teacher, and then said, "Are my Active Christians here? Paul and Mike and—er——" He picked them out and oozed up the aisle to them, seating himself on a desk. "I just popped down to see how you were getting on—shall I be seeing you at the meeting tonight?"

Tony said, "I can't manage it."

Mike shuffled his feet, and said, "I've got to go out with me Mom and Dad."

"Oh dear. What about you Paul?"

"I dunno," Paul said. He stared blankly at the teacher, and Mr Archer did not press the point. "Have you visited your people since Thursday?"

No answer. Mr Archer sighed, and stood up. "Well, boys— I hope you haven't forgotten them. I'll be dropping in on them tonight, to keep them with us. . . ."

Paul made a mental note not to call in on Mrs Maxwell, as he'd been meaning to, and they slid away.

The path from the door to the foot-bridge across the main road was long, and they dawdled, chatting and laughing. Paul walked backwards in front of Tony and Mike, crowing over his baiting of Mr Ward. They saw his face change. Then he turned his back and ran.

From behind came a soaring cry of "Mentor! I'll get you!" They looked, and saw Mal, running hard, his knees coming up by his chest, his blazer flying. He left the path and ran across the field to cut Paul off.

But Paul skimmed like a bird, covering the ground with amazing speed. Mal pumped past Mike and Tony, breathing hard as he slowed for the bank of the field.

"Run, Paul, run!" Mike yelled, as Paul gained the steps of the bridge. They watched Paul springing up the steps of the bridge as if pulled from above, while Mal hadn't yet reached the gate from the school grounds, which Paul had slammed shut behind him. By the time he had the gate open and was climbing the steps, Paul had disappeared.

Mike and Tony ran up to the fence, watching eagerly, and cheered as Paul reappeared on the opposite side of the road, still running. Hoorooing, they ran up on to the bridge, where they found Mal, bent over with the stitch.

"What was all that about?" Tony asked. "What's going on?"

"That little bastard," Mal panted. "I'll kill him!"

"What's he done?"

"Only—only marked me absent—for weeks! I got detention all this week for messing up the register—oh, go on—laugh, why don't you!"

Tony did, but Mike could ask, "Why didn't you tell 'em it was Paul?"

"Oh ar! They wouldn't believe me, would they? I can just hear meself explaining that. I ain't saft!"

They crossed the bridge, and could see Paul, still in top gear, in the distance.

"Christ," Mike said. "Can't he run though?"

Chapter Five

Paul found his own way to school the next day, in order to avoid Mal, and was careful to avoid him all that day. He wasn't really worried; he didn't think that Mal would bear a grudge for long, and he wouldn't do more than cuff Paul's head anyway, but the cloak and dagger stuff around the school added spice to life. Tuesday was a very boring day.

All Paul's worst subjects. Two lessons of Maths in the morning, right after dodging Assembly. Eighty minutes of Maths; the mere thought left him so depressed that he hadn't even the energy to disturb the lesson.

And then two lessons of French. After five years of French lessons, Paul still couldn't string two subjunctives together. It was all a foreign language to him, and he collected more thumps over the head with heavy books than anyone else in the class.

After dinner, a lesson of Geography, which Paul, and everyone else, found almost too tedious to bear. Even the teacher spoke in a bored monotone. They looked at diagrams of cocoa-pods, and black and white photographs of factory plants, and discussed the annual rainfall of the Balkan States. Paul sighed, and looked at his watch.

The only highlight of the day was the final two lessons of art. After all the other lessons, it was like breaking out of prison. The art room was large and light, with many single desks. The lids of the desks could be stood up to make easels, and the body held paints and water-jars. Paul went into the art room whooping like a Huron, and headed straight for the cupboard where the folders of art-work were kept.

"Paul," Mr Grade said. "Not today."

Paul sat back on his heels in front of the cupboard, with its door open. "Oh, sir—I want to finish me picture."

"And I want to give a lesson on composition and design," Mr Grade said. He was a short man, not much taller than Paul, and about fifty years old, with frizzy hair. "Come on—everybody—round the board, round the board," he said, as the rest of the class began to fill the room.

"But, sir—I *know* about composition and design," Paul said, clutching his folder hopefully.

"Oh, *do* you?" Mr Grade said, raising himself on his toes and opening his eyes very wide. "Who says so?"

"You did, sir. You said I had an unconscious grasp of the principles of design."

Mr Grade's face did not change. "I did, did I?" he nodded. "What're you doing now? Bring it here and let me see."

Paul hurriedly sorted through his folder, pulled out a large sheet of paper and took it across to the teacher. Mr Grade spread it across a desk, and studied it, while other members of the class leaned over to look at it.

It was a long picture, showing a silver space-ship passing a ringed planet. Many colours were splashed on without finishing it, but it already had depth. Mr Grade looked at it for a long time, then said, "All right. You can go to the back of the class and paint—providing you're quiet and don't disturb the rest of the class."

"Yes, sir, I will, sir," Paul said. "Thank you, sir," he added. Mr Grade was the only teacher in the school for whom he had a real respect, besides liking.

The rest of the class settled, with sighs, to a boring lesson; but most of them found art boring anyway, so it didn't make much difference.

"I've been looking at your work, and I find that most of you know nothing at all of the basic principles of design. I don't know what your other teachers have been doing these past few years, but——" Mr Grade was off, working up to his usual harangue. Paul listened at first, with half an ear, but was then absorbed in his painting.

He was using polyester paints. They were expensive, and Paul was the only person outside the Sixth Form allowed to use them. A plastic paint, they could be used like water colours or oils, or even mixed with a plastic glue to form a coloured glaze. Their disadvantage was that they dried in a very short time, a few minutes, and couldn't be softened for re-use. Paul had a plate and palette knife from the cookery department to mix them with, and a tube of sticky glue. He was at his happiest, whistling and swearing, scowling with concentration; his mind filled with what the picture should look like, and his hands struggling to deal with what it was like.

At four o'clock the picture was as good as finished. There were one or two details that could be added, some small corrections to be made, but Paul was satisfied that it was as good as he could make it for the moment. In a few days' time he would probably think differently, but he would have lost interest in it by that time anyway, and be painting something else. He rolled the painting up and took it with him, not to show his parents, but to show Mrs Maxwell. He didn't leave the school grounds by the bridge but by the main gates, thereby avoiding Mal and cutting a corner off his walk. He went up to the main road, a busy dual carriageway, crossed to the centre reservation and walked along it, between the lorries and the cars, waiting for a gap to run through. Then it was the steep climb to the street where Mrs Maxwell lived.

He reached the door of the little house, laid his hand on the smooth knob—and waited a breath of time. To let the house behind the door come together and solidify. When he opened the door, there the room would be, faded and yellow, and the back of Mrs Maxwell's chair, where she would be sitting, wrapped in her tartan shawl. And he would make a cup of tea.

He turned the knob and shoved open the door, going in smartly. The plastic cloth had been taken from the table, and the linen cloth shone. A steaming teapot was set on a mat, with a sugar-bowl and milk-jug, and a teacup on a saucer. The fire was burning up, and the whole room looked different, lighter, brighter; less like Mrs Maxwell's house and more like his own.

Her chair was empty. He ran into the kitchen, and she wasn't there. He opened the door on to the yard, and she wasn't there either. The door of the outside lavatory stood open. He wandered back, into the living-room, and stood on the hearth, not knowing what to do, and filled with a reasonless fear that something had happened to her. She was lying somewhere with a broken leg—he should go and look for her—steam rose from the teapot's spout.

Then he heard heavy footsteps from within the wall. From the stairs. He jumped across the room and opened the stairdoor. There was Mrs Maxwell coming down, one step at a time, very slowly.

"Hello, love!" she said, and smiled. Paul thought: She's really pleased to see me, and grinned back with a little gasp of pleasure. "I thought you weren't coming any more." She reached the bottom of the stairs, and Paul gave her his arm to help her off the last big step and into the room. "I thought you'd be coming yesterday, but you didn't. That man did, and he said you'd be coming later on, but you never did." She was wheezing and panting again, and Paul said quickly:

"Come and sit down."

"I told him how you'd come and done me shopping and made me fires, though, that man, and he said he needn't come again then. I'm glad, I didn't like him."

"Yes," Paul said. "Come and sit down."

But, determined as a tortoise, she then started for the

kitchen door, and he didn't like to pull at her arm in case he hurt her. She went into the kitchen, and took a cup and saucer for him from the dresser, and two little plates. Back she started for the table in the living-room. Paul could have done both trips in half the time it took her to do one.

"Sit down," he begged her again, but she ignored him. Shuffling over to the sideboard, she stooped in a series of jerks and opened one of the cupboards, taking out a biscuit box. She prised the lid off and filled both little plates with home-made cakes. Paul stared at them.

"I made 'em yesterday," Mrs Maxwell said. "I thought you'd be coming, you see. They would have been warm from the oven. When I thought you weren't coming any more, I put 'em up, I thought I could just have one now and then." But he had come, and she plainly expected him to eat the whole boxful.

"Thanks," he said, but uncomfortably. He couldn't fit his idea of Mrs Maxwell to this busy little body, making cakes and pouring tea.

"*I'll* pour the tea," Paul said. "Come and sit down."

But no, she must pour a little milk from the milk-jug into each cup, and balance the tea-strainer on them, and pour the tea—"How many spoons, love?"

For the first time Paul noticed that the cups were the thin white ones with pink flowers painted inside, that the jugs matched them, and the plates. He understood. He was being entertained.

"Er—I don't like—take sugar," he said. "Thank you."

So she sugared her own tea, and pulled out one of the straight-backed chairs. It was to be a formal entertainment, and that Paul couldn't take.

"No, come and sit by the fire," he said. "I'll pass you your tea. Come on." And he took her cup of tea from the table and put it on the hob of the range.

"Oh, all right," she said, smiling.

He smoothed the cushions of her chair, and took her arm to help her across the room, and put the tartan shawl around her shoulders, and knelt to put a footstool under her feet, and stood to put her cup into her hand—stirring it first—and she seemed vastly amused by it all. But he had her how he wanted her now, as she should have been when he came in. He brought her plate of cakes, and sat himself on another footstool on the hearth, with his tea and plate. As he bit into one of the cakes, he noticed how old her slippers were, and how one was split. A picture slid into his mind of the blue fluffy slippers crushed into the corner of the living-room at home. They belonged to his mother or his sister; he didn't know which, but they were never worn.

The cakes were moist, and soft, and full of chocolate bits. "My Mom doesn't make cakes," he said, and after another bite, "These am better than you get out the shops."

"I always used to make cakes," she said. "Big bon-fulls of 'em. All kinds. They used to go through 'em in no time."

Paul wondered vaguely who "they" were, but didn't really want to know. He remembered his painting, and got up to fetch it from where he had dropped it. He unrolled it across the floor at her feet, holding it down. "Look," he said. "I did this at school today."

She looked at it for a long time: the weirdly shadowed, clouded planet with its rings of light; the space-ship, slightly lop-sided, but still impressive with its reflected colours; the darkness of space, which was not black, but blue and green and dark red.

"Very good," she said. "What is it?"

"It's a space-ship," he said. "Like in *2001*. Like the Apollos they sent to the moon."

She nodded wisely. "Mmm," she said. "Did you do it?"

"Yes! I did it at school. With polyester paints. See, you can't get colours like these with water-paints. Not them at school anyway, where all the little kids have been messin' 'em about."

"Our Jeff used to paint."

"Who's Jeff?" Paul asked.

"Jeff? Me grandson. Our Eric's lad."

Paul immediately hated Jeff, dead as he might be. Alive, Paul would bet he had never painted as well as he could; dead, he had no right to be honoured with the title of "grandson". "Did he? What did he paint then?"

"Oh, him," the old lady said. "It was painting one week and motor-bikes the next. He never settled to anythin'." She put her cup on the hob and heaved herself out of her chair. "I'll show you," she said. "Got a picture of his upstairs."

Paul got up quickly. "I'll fetch it."

She chuckled. "You don't know where it is."

"You could tell me," but she ignored him. So he followed her up the steep, dark stairs, to save her from falling if she slipped, although she climbed very slowly and solidly. On the little square landing at the top, he could hear her panting.

"You shouldn't climb up and down the stairs," he said sternly. "I could have come."

"I've climbed up and down these stairs all me life," she said, and went up a step into a bedroom, switching on the light.

It was a dismal room. The divan bed was stripped to the mattress, and piled with old cardboard boxes. There was a dressing-table covered with nothing but dust, and a carpet; that was all. Paul had been expecting a room kept just as Jeff had left it, as in all good books, and he was relieved rather than disappointed. "Our Eric and Sam slept in here when they was lads," Mrs Maxwell said, "and then Jeff had it." She rolled across to the bed, Paul at her elbow. As she moved the boxes clouds of dust arose and made him cough. She found a large, flat chocolate box and took off the lid. Inside were lines and lines of oil paints, all in tubes with labels showing their colour, all sizes, all colours. And a real palette. And fistfuls of brushes, thin and fat and medium. And a bottle of linseed oil, and a bottle of turpentine.

"Strewth," Paul said. He had never seen such a wonderful sight, even at school. The hoard must have cost pounds altogether.

"Here's one of his paintings," Mrs Maxwell said. She unfolded a piece of paper and laid it on the bed. It wasn't half finished. In heavy pencil there was drawn a field, a tree, something which might have been a cow, and some hills in the distance. These distant hills had been painted a muddy green.

"He never finished it," she said, and Paul heard the question.

"I could finish it for you," he answered, "if you like." He pulled out more paintings, some done on hardboard. Flowers in a vase, a woman sitting in a chair, a sunset. Paul didn't think any of them very good, and gloated over his own talent.

"You could finish it, if you liked," Mrs Maxwell said.

If he liked. He looked over all those tubes again, and almost licked his lips. He had never before done any painting in his own time, only at school, but here, in this house, it was different. He'd been asked to. Mrs Maxwell wanted the picture finishing.

He put the lid back on the box, refolded the paper on top of it, and picked it up. "I'll go down first," he said. Then, if she slipped, she wouldn't fall any further than him.

Despite the fact that Paul couldn't see where he was going for the box held in front of him, they both got down the stairs safely. Mrs Maxwell poured herself another cup of tea and switched on the radio, while Paul dropped down on the hearth and opened up the box. As soon as he had a splash of green squeezed out on to the palette he realized that he didn't know how to use oil paints. There might be some special way he ought to know about.

He turned the paints over, disappointed, and discovered beneath them a grubby little booklet. Crosslegged he sat and read it. It described the properties of oil paints, how they can be used to paint directly over another colour, how they can be used as they come from the tube, or thinned with a mixture of linseed oil and turps, made glossy with linseed oil or dull and flat with turpentine. It said that bright colours should be used because it was easier to deaden colours than brighten them. Then there was a list of instructions on how to mix certain colours, such as "sun-tanned skin" and "hay-field", which Paul didn't bother to read.

Armed with this new knowledge he set out to finish the painting. He asked Mrs Maxwell for something to mix the linseed and turps in, and she gave him an egg-cup and some old newspapers to go under the painting, and to lay the brushes on. Looking at the painting he was tempted to turn it into an eerie Jovian landscape of sulphurous plains and obsidian mountains; to transform the cow into a slate-blue, twelve-foot-tall, eight-legged, red-eyed Gronk. It didn't look much like a cow anyway. But he thought the old lady wouldn't like it; after all, it was her grandson's painting she wanted finished.

So he took a big brush and painted in sky. He did it white and blue, like summer, and very quickly. It looked skyish enough, so he didn't tempt fate and left it. Then he repainted the distant hills in a tawny colour, altering their line a little. He made the colour greener as it came downhill, until it was lush in the field. He tried to make it look deep, like long grass. He painted a tree where Jeff had indicated one, and put in another for the look of it. The cow he painted over in the field and found, to his delight, that you could use one colour directly over another, while they were still wet. He tried to make the cow a Jersey cow, but he wasn't very good at cows. Better than Jeff though. He sat back on his heels and looked at it. It was a very boring picture, but he had enjoyed the painting.

"I've finished," he said, and was surprised to find how tired he was, and hungry.

"Well, I don't know," Mrs Maxwell said. "I thought you'd

gone home, you've been so quiet. I'll bet your mother knows how to keep you out of her hair."

"No," Paul said, and sighed, and stretched. He turned the painting round on the floor and said, "Look."

She did. "That is lovely," she said, and started to get out of her chair. "That is lovely. I shall pin it on the wall."

"It won't be dry for three weeks," Paul said, but she was up and sorting through the sideboard drawers. Paul took up the heavy piece of paper, and laid it on the table, and when she turned round with a box of drawing-pins, he said, "You'll have to wait until it's dry first. And I'll get it mounted then." He grinned with excitement and pride because she *would* have pinned it up. Not on a school wall, but on *her* wall, because she liked it. "I'll take all the paints and everything upstairs, and it can dry up there."

He tidied up, and packed the paints in their box, and took them and the picture upstairs to the empty bedroom. Coming back down again, he saw the time on the clock on the mantelpiece. Twenty past ten.

"The time!" he said. "I'd better be goin'." But first he filled the box on the hearth with wood and coal.

"I'll get it mounted when it's dry and you can pin it up," he assured her. "It'll be like a proper picture."

"Lovely," she said. "You be careful how you go now."

Outside it was dark and cool, and Paul was grateful for it, walking slowly. Tomorrow he would really paint her a picture, one of his own, not of Jeff's—he stopped when he realized he'd left the space-ship picture behind. It should be at school, to be judged as part of his term's work. Ah well, he could collect it tomorrow. He walked home, and went straight up to bed.

He did go to see Mrs Maxwell the next day, and found that she'd pinned the space-ship picture up on her wall, instead of Jeff's cow in the field. With its size and colour and depth it hit him as soon as he walked through the door, and for a second he could hardly believe that he'd painted it. It looked great. And it was certainly one in the eye for Jeff.

That night Mrs Maxwell toasted pikelets at the range-fire while Paul sat on the hearth and made sketches, on Jeff's paper, for the masterpiece that would lay Jeff for ever. Mrs Maxwell talked while he drew, talked about Jeff and gave Paul more reason to hate him. He'd been a good boy, Jeff, always ready to help her. He'd always done the shopping. Motor-bike mad, though; about the only one of his crazes that had lasted. He'd been mad about—oh, speedway one week, and stock cars the next; then he was going to emigrate to Australia like his uncle, and then he was going to be a salesman—Mrs Maxwell laughed about his enthusiasms, but Paul thought he must have been stupid. Paul was implacably, immovably set against Jeff and everything he had done, and said.

He asked the old lady to sit still while he drew her. She thought it was a wonderful idea, but she wouldn't keep still. She had to keep striking poses, and then, in the middle of his sketching, got up to fetch a hat from the kitchen, a round black hat with a big pearly pin. She sat down again with the hat tilted to the back of her head. Paul had to alter his sketch.

When it was finished, she laughed and admired it a good deal, saying that the face in the picture was much too pretty to be her. Paul said it wasn't pretty enough, and she called him a flirt. She pinned the drawing up beside the fireplace, and made Paul's day, but he didn't allow himself to be flattered out of all judgement. The picture wasn't a bad likeness, but the head was a bit lop-sided.

Still, she gave him a chance to do better, for when he looked up a little time after, when there'd been quiet between them for a while, he saw that she'd fallen asleep. He quickly changed his footstool for a straight-backed chair and, balancing the pad on his knee, made another drawing of her. The result was a portrait that satisfied him as a drawing, but not as a likeness. Still, you couldn't have everything. He pinned it up beside the first picture, and then was very quiet because Mrs Maxwell was still asleep.

He decided on the painting he was going to do for her, a Norse-god type with a flaring cloak of many colours, ascending through the nebulae and galaxies of space. But he didn't get a chance to start it because the next day the weather turned cold again, and Mrs Maxwell's rheumatism played her up. So Paul was busy when he called on her. He filled her fuel box, and cooked her a boiled egg with toast, which he cut into fingers for easier handling. While she ate he searched the empty bedroom above and found a large hot-water bottle which she said she thought she'd put there. He filled it, and put it into her bed, then went down again and washed the plate and egg-cup. He helped her upstairs, and put a raker on the fire, a piece of coal in which the strata ran horizontally, to keep the fire alight until morning.

And for the next week or so he did the housework, ran errands, made fires, cooked meals, made the bed. He even, at Mrs Maxwell's especial request, scrubbed the front doorstep, a thing he would never have thought of doing himself, and wouldn't have done for anyone else. Nothing was too much trouble, because he enjoyed the praise the old lady heaped on his head, and because he was working hard at replacing Jeff. If she offered to help, he would insist fiercely and continuously that she should go back to her chair and sit down.

She said he was like a mother-hen, which insulted him so much that he stayed away for two days.

But the thought of her waiting for him to come, and then being disappointed, tortured him for most of the first day and all of the second, and on the third he knocked at her door bearing gifts—the pair of fluffy blue slippers from the corner of the living-room at home.

The room was cold inside, and Mrs Maxwell sat in her armchair, huddled in her tartan shawl. There was no fire, and she was dressed only in her nightdress and an old cardigan. She smiled stiffly at him.

For a moment Paul had thought she was dead, and his heart had stopped and turned sick within him. "How long have you been sitting here?" he asked, but she didn't answer, and Paul realized that he should get her warm as soon as possible. What was the quickest way? His mind scuttled round like a white mouse in a wheel.

"Come on," he said, "up to bed." He bent down and took hold of her round the waist. He pulled. She was heavier than he'd thought, and she was stiff with the cold. He let her go. If he got her out of the chair, she wouldn't be able to get upstairs.

"I'll make a fire!" he said. Half-way to the coal-hole, he remembered the hot-water bottle, ran into the kitchen and put the kettle on, then ran up the stairs to fetch the bottle. While the kettle boiled, he filled the fuel-box, ready to make a fire.

The kettle boiled, he ran a little cold water into the bottle, then filled it from the kettle. It was still very hot, and he changed it from arm to arm as he carried it into the other room, and wrapped it in the linen cloth from the table. He put it into her arms, and tucked it in with her with the heavy velvet table-cloth and his jacket. Then he began on the fire.

Piling up wood and paper, he almost wept. The fire might not catch, anyhow it would take a long time to burn up, and the hot-water bottle might not be enough. She might be getting colder and colder all the time. She might have died, might have died, and it would have been all his fault. "I'm sorry," he kept saying. "I won't leave you again. I'll *always* come in future, I promise."

When he at last had the fire burning he knelt before her chair and stared anxiously into her face. She didn't look well, she didn't look at all well, and tears came up over his lashes. Maybe she was like that old lady in the telly advert who gets colder and colder until she dies. Maybe he was too late. "Are you all *right*?" he asked. She smiled at him again.

"I'll make a cup of tea!" he said, and went into the kitchen to put the kettle on again. He was relieved to see, when the tea was made, that she was well enough to reach out for her cup. "Are you hungry?" Paul asked. "Shall I cook you something?"

She shook her head.

"I won't not come again," Paul assured her solemnly, shaking his head. "I'll always come. Every night. Honest. I promise."

He knelt at the arm of her chair, watching her face for signs of collapse, or heart-attack, or creeping death, but what he would do, even should he recognize such signs, he had no idea.

But some of her colour returned, and the first thing she said was, "You're a good boy."

"How long have you been sitting in the cold like this?" Paul asked.

Her voice was a croak. She said, "If you go and look in that drawer, you'll find something for yourself."

Paul crossed to the sideboard and opened the top drawer. Floating on top of the jumble was a red and yellow sugar lollipop. "Thank you," he said.

"I'd like to go back to bed now, I think," Mrs Maxwell said.

So he helped her upstairs and into bed, tartan shawl, cardigan and all, and tucked her in with her hot-water bottle. Then he was afraid to leave her. She might get cold again, and die in the night. So, although it might have been better for her to get some sleep, he sat on the bed and talked to her. He told her about school and about his friends; and she became talkative enough to tell him about her husband, who had been a breadman and a drunk, by all accounts. She said he'd died of cancer, but judging from the stories, Paul thought it was more likely to have been cirrhosis of the liver. And then she asked him if his mother would mind his being out so late.

Paul was sensitive to veiled hints, and stood up, saying, "Do you want me to go now?"

But it turned out that what Mrs Maxwell had really meant was, what kind of a person was his mother?

Paul was stuck for an answer. He thought for some time as they shared the lollipop, suck and suck about, and came up with, "She's good-lookin', I suppose. She smokes. She goes out to work as well." The old lady waited expectantly for stories, as she'd told stories about her husband. But none came. Paul couldn't think of any.

"Where does she work?" the old lady asked, prompting him.

After a moment's pause, he said, "She makes screws. She gets bits of curly metal in her fingers."

"Doesn't she mind you coming to see me every night?"

"No," Paul said, truthfully as it happened, because his mother didn't know anything about Mrs Maxwell.

"Doesn't she mind you staying out so late? Doesn't she worry?"

Paul genuinely considered the question, and answered as truthfully as he could. "No. I'm fifteen. Why should she?"

They talked on, until Mrs Maxwell fell asleep. It was then twenty to eleven, but Paul still didn't want to leave.

He was afraid to leave, because he was convinced that, in the last resort, only his presence kept the dark from the house. He didn't want to leave her alone in the dark. But he had to go home. If he didn't go home terrible consequences would be unleashed; mother and father furious, police searches, explanations, thumpings . . . especially thumpings.

He compromised. He would come back early in the morning, before school. If he came back as soon as he could, perhaps everything would still be all right.

He was back at half-past seven the next morning. Anxiety had not let him sleep long. He stayed all day.

Chapter Six

He hadn't gone to Mrs Maxwell's intending to play the wag from school. It just turned out that way. She seemed to expect him to stay. She sent him to buy biscuits from the corner shop, and they spent the time in talking and laughing, and talking some more.

Paul learned more about her drunken husband and her two sons, Eric and Sam, how they used to fight with each other and argue all day long. They made funny stories, like the time she had got between them to stop a fight, and caught a fist in the eye instead. Mrs Maxwell told how Sam had gone to Australia, and they never heard from him again, and how Eric had married a girl not good enough for him.

It was all fascinating to Paul; all the old situations, all the old phrases, stock from a television soap-box serial, had suddenly come to life. It was better than any film or book.

Mrs Maxwell had not been lucky with her family. Some people just seemed to have bad luck. He had heard his mother tell of similar families, but had never known the people himself. Now Mrs Maxwell went on to say how her son, Eric, had been killed. He'd been crossing a hump-backed bridge one day when a bus had come along and smeared him the length of the parapet. His widow then proved her worthlessness by finding herself a "fancy-man", unloading young Jeff on his gran, and going off herself to live in Rhyl over a rock-shop, and never writing.

"Didn't she—didn't she ever send him a card or nothin'?" Paul asked, enthralled, from his footstool.

"She never sent him or me a card, nor a letter, nor a present, not from the day her left, not even a stick of rock," said the old lady, with emphasis.

"Strewth!" Paul said.

In exchange, he tried to tell her about himself, and his family, but his life had been markedly less interesting, and he found it difficult to describe his relatives. Of his father he could only say, "He's a big man. Stiff—fat, you know. He watches the football sometimes." And of his sister, "She's a girl—tall girl, you know. Goes out a lot."

He found it much easier to tell her about his friends, and she heard all about what a smart-alec Mal was, how he thought he knew everything; and how Tony was the strongest boy in the form, acknowledged champion of the fifth year. And what a dope Mike was.

More shyly he mentioned some girls, with the recommendation, "Her's nice." He would have said why she was nice, but feared to offend the old lady. Mrs Maxwell smiled wisely in her shawl.

Paul was rarely bored at Mrs Maxwell's house. He listened for hours to her telling of when she'd been a girl. He'd always been told before of how peaceful were the days before the motor-car, but Mrs Maxwell said that the cart-wheels had been iron-rimmed and had made a terrible din on the cobbles, worse than any lorry; and that if anyone in the street was ill, the whole neighbourhood would throw down straw and sacks in the road, to muffle the noise. She told of all the rows and squabbles that had gone on in a tiny house filled with ten people, of how in the midst of all the turmoil her mother had found room for a box of ducklings, and of how the birds would escape and run all over the house with everyone chasing them. She told him of things he wouldn't have imagined possible a mere sixty or seventy years ago. While they giggled like six-year-olds, she described their toilets, a box with a hole in the top, and a bucket underneath, which had to be emptied frequently. He heard of doctors who charged twelve and a half pence just to come and say there was nothing wrong with you, and that, in those days, seventy-five pence might be a man's whole wage for a week.

"Nothing good about them, was there, the old days?" Paul said.

"Oh, no," said Mrs Maxwell. "We had some good times." And she went on to tell of home-made bread, crusty and hot from the range-oven, so that the butter melted on it—but, of course, they had dripping most of the time. But the meat! The meat, stewed in jars in the oven, was lovely, so tender and sweet. And then there was the theatre, the Variety Palace. The laughs they had there! There'd be a puff of blue smoke, and a ghostly, flapping sheet would rise up from behind a settee, while the audience roared with laughter, or chewed their nails with fear, according to how many times they had seen the plays. Oh, and the Clutching Hand, reaching from behind the curtains—"And Shakespeare," Mrs Maxwell said. "Oh yes, I'm not ignorant, you know. Oh, no."

"*You* don't know any Shakespeare," Paul teased her. "They wouldn't waste *Him* on you."

" 'Your only jig-maker,' " the old lady said cryptically. " 'What should a man do but be merry? How cheerfully my mother looks and my father died within this two hours.' What's that then, if it ain't Shakespeare?"

"I dunno. The Clutching Hand's exit line?" Paul asked.

" 'Course, it was hard work for the women in them days," Mrs Maxwell said. "My poor mother. When I think of all her had to do . . . with eight childer. 'Cos there was none of these washing-machines an'—an' vacuum-cleaners then, you know. It all had to be done by hand. By the women." And she explained how the boiler had to be filled for the weekly wash the night before the washing was done, by carrying bucket after heavy bucket across the yard from the pump, and of how the actual washing was done with a block of wood called a maid, banging it up and down on the clothes in the tub, and with a scrubbing-board, both jobs being very hard work. Then there were meals to cook for eight people, and a week's supply of bread to be baked, floors to be scrubbed, yes, and the step, every week; and the range to be blackleaded, darning and mending to be done, the floors swept, the crocks washed, the furniture to be dusted, shopping to be done, no time for sitting about. "We hadn't got much money," Mrs Maxwell said proudly, "but you could have et your dinner off the floor or the sideboard, or anywhere in our house. Her kept it spotless, my mother did. Her worked herself away. You don't see women working like that now, oh no. It's all frozen foods and sliced bread, and take the washing down to the 'launderette', I've seen 'em. The women had hard life then."

"And the men," Paul protested. "They wasn't sitting about eating strawberries and cream, was they?"

"Oh no," said Mrs Maxwell. "No. They worked hard an' all. They didn't go on strike, neither, and they worked longer hours for less. My father now, he was chain-maker. He'd a beer belly on him. He worked every hour God sent and drank the rest. He got thirsty, see, in his line of work." But Mrs Maxwell seemed far more concerned with the hardships women suffered.

Whatever stories she chose to tell, Paul drank it all in. The stories were like the old skulls and coins in museums; they had the same quality of having been real or true once, but in a world and time Paul could know nothing of. They reminded him again of the vast gap between him and Mrs Maxwell, which he often forgot, for she seemed closer to him than—well, than his parents, certainly, and often closer than his friends of his own age. Everything he spoke of, she seemed to have known herself. He supposed it was because she had seen it all before, from all angles; she'd had brothers, and sons, and a grandson; been a sister, wife, mother and grandmother. Just sometimes she seemed less experienced than him too. Well, she did have less experience in his world. But he didn't try to understand it all.

If she didn't want to talk, Paul would sometimes do homework. There was a comfortable quiet in the old lady's house which helped his concentration, he thought. At home, there was either a roaring from the television set, and people shouting above it, or a dead, heavy silence that made you want to get up and make or hunt for some noise. In Mrs Maxwell's house there was never silence, just quiet. If they weren't talking, there was the fire whispering and crackling to itself, the clock ticking solemnly high above their heads on the mantelpiece, the stairs and walls creaking, and a high-pitched humming sound which Mrs Maxwell said you always heard if you were quiet, and listened for it.

At other times Paul would draw or paint. It had become a habit, sketching and doodling at odd moments, and not just during a certain lesson at school. But still he only drew at Mrs Maxwell's house, where he had the paper and pencils. He did more painting too, he even thought of buying some new paints when Jeff's ran out, and keeping them at Mrs Maxwell's house. He realized that there was much more variety in the pictures and paintings pinned around Mrs Maxwell's walls than in his art-work folder at school. There were sketches of Mrs Maxwell and of her room and of the back-yard, and paintings of streets and cars and people, besides space-ships, alien landscapes and monsters. Probably because here he didn't have to hold up his reputation by doing only things which he knew he could do well, anything and everything he did was praised fulsomely by Mrs Maxwell. She thought they were all wonderful.

"The car isn't exactly right," Paul would excuse himself. "The wheels am a bit too small for a start."

Mrs Maxwell would peer at the picture closely, but how

much she actually saw Paul couldn't be sure. After a couple of minutes, she would say, "It looks all right to me. It's a beautiful picture. Where's the pins? Put it up over there."

When the weather grew a little warmer, Mrs Maxwell bought some seeds from the corner shop for nine pence a packet, expecting, without asking, that Paul would dig over her bit of garden and plant them for her. Paul, when handed the packets, saw at once what a cheek and a diabolical liberty she was taking; but he was grateful. No one had ever paid him such a compliment, it was even better than having his pictures pinned up. He was so eager to repay her for this kindness that he started on the garden that night, and skipped school the next day to get on with it. The old fork and spade he found propped behind the lavatory were a little big for him, and the ground hadn't been dug for some years, and so the work tended to be done in short bursts, but it got done, and one fine spring night, with a soft breeze blowing gently from the chemical works, Paul planted the seeds, cabbage and carrots and turnips, while Mrs Maxwell watched from the back door-step, wrapped in her tartan shawl.

"What we need," Paul said, sitting back on his heels, "is some fertilizer."

"We don't need fertilizer," Mrs Maxwell said, in a voice of scorn. She snuffed the air loudly. "Smell that? Get some of that across your chest. Sulphur, that is, and phossie. All you need to grow good veg, that is. 'Course, a gas-works brings on rhubarb better."

Paul stared. "What—really?" he said, trying to assess this new information in the light of recent Biology lessons on soil humus and chlorophyll in plants.

Mrs Maxwell stood and watched him for a time, as if suspecting him of joking too. Then she laughed, with her head back.

"Anyway," Paul said loudly, coming to the step, brushing his damp hair from his eyes, "one thing I am going to do."

"What's that, my love?"

"Get some cans and sticks and make a bird-scarer. I don't want no ruddy birds stuffin' all them seeds after I worked so hard with 'em."

"Well, an' you have worked hard an' all," Mrs Maxwell said. "You go in an' sit down, an' I'll put the kettle on."

"What?" Paul exclaimed indignantly. "*You* go and sit down, and *I'll* put the kettle on."

At other times, there were household chores to be done. The washing-up and cooking were easy enough, since there were only Mrs Maxwell and himself, but on one occasion Paul tried his hand at blackleading the grate and looked, Mrs Maxwell said, like a nigger minstrel when he'd finished. He had to wash before he went home. There was the washing too. Mrs Maxwell still washed a lot of her things by hand in the sink; her knuckles were worn flat with rubbing; but she couldn't manage things like sheets and curtains, and sometimes her rheumatism was too bad for her to do any washing at all. Paul knew nothing about washing and didn't fancy learning, but he was sure that he could use one of the machines at the launderette just down the road. He suggested it, but Mrs Maxwell said that she couldn't afford two shillings every wash. Neither could Paul, but he devised a way to find the money. It was simple. He went without school-dinners for a couple of days, ate bread and jam at Mrs Maxwell's instead, and washed her clothes with the money his mother gave him for his school-dinners.

It was about the same time that his trips to the launderette were becoming regular that *Planet of the Apes* came to the local picture house. Paul wanted to see it. Mal didn't, and Tony followed his lead. Mike said it was daft.

Paul didn't much like going to the pictures on his own, the more the merrier was his motto, and so he went with Mrs Maxwell instead. On a Wednesday afternoon, when it was half-price for old age pensioners. Paul paid for them both, from his pound pocket-money; it only cost sixty-one pence for the two tickets. The outing was a great success, and Mrs Maxwell was much impressed with the film.

"However did they get them great big monkeys to act like that?" she asked when they came out. Paul laughed nervously. He could still never be sure of when she was joking and when she was serious.

After that, there seemed to be something good on at the pictures every other week. He would look up the advertisements in the local weekend papers, and if the programme was good, would save his pocket-money until Wednesday. He would pay for the seats, and Mrs Maxwell would bring sweets from the corner shop. Sitting in the stalls, Mrs Maxwell clutching her handbag, and Paul with his feet on the seats in front, almost lying on his back, they sucked on sherbert-suckers, licked lollipops, devoured jelly-lizards and gnawed at banana toffee while the films flooded the screen above them. Mrs Maxwell liked the car chases and the fights best, squealing with excitement as the cars leaped bridges with all four wheels in the air or men fell bullet-riddled from roof-tops. Paul preferred the comedies and the police stories, and the revivals that the local cinema put on, like *Flash Gordon*.

Paul enjoyed the afternoons at the pictures, but at school the situation was becoming difficult. He was an expert at keeping teachers waiting for excuse-notes: "I'll tell me Mom she'll have to write one, sir. . . . Oh, I left it on the shelf, sir. . . . I forgot it again, sir, I'll bring it tomorrow. . . . Me Mom burnt it, sir, she thought I didn't need it any more, I'll get her to write another . . . she hasn't written it yet, sir. . . . I'll bring it tomorrow. . . ." But the teacher was becoming insistent. So Paul sat down at Mrs Maxwell's house and wrote his own excuse-notes. He knew that he would have to be careful.

But now the weather grew steadily warmer, with fresh, bright days that it was torture to spend in classrooms. He was tempted. On a Thursday afternoon, when lessons were dull, he took Mrs Maxwell to the park, where they fed pigeons under the fountain's spray, and he picked her a bunch of daffodils while no one was looking. Another week he dragged her out to the Zoo, and threw pebbles at the lions to make them growl, and she said, "Goodness gracious me!" He looked back at the lions as they went on to the kangaroos. They lay in great heaps, like ash-burned hearth-rugs, over the rocks in their pit. They were just like people, you had to throw things at them to get any kind of reaction at all.

Mrs Maxwell never wanted to come on these outings when he first asked her, because she'd sat in her house for so long, but afterwards, with a cup of tea, sitting in her chair, she'd say she enjoyed herself. Paul enjoyed them too, although he couldn't think why. They were so tame. Feeding pigeons, watching goldfish swim in a muddy pool, talking to a mynah-bird in a pet-shop which said, "Cheeky!", "Show us a leg", "Nice to see you" and something in Spanish which no one understood, but which the shop-keeper thought was probably rude. Paul fancied himself a Socrates, and evolved a philosophy which said that all you needed for true happiness was the opportunity to stroll round a parrot-cage in the sun.

He had thought that his visits to Mrs Maxwell were a dark secret, known only to himself and her, but he found otherwise. It was while he was attacking the grime on the outside of the living-room windows with a bottle of Windowlene and some filthy rags, that the woman next door spoke to him. Stooping to set an empty milk-bottle on her step, she said slowly, "Hello."

"Hello," Paul said, and smiled at her.

The woman leaned against the jamb of her door. She wore slippers, and curlers in her hair, and was quite attractive, although about thirty. "What's your name, love?"

Paul glanced up at her, squinting against the bright, late sunlight which came down the street. He wondered what she wanted. "Paul Mentor. What's yours?"

She laughed and said, "Dora—Dora, that's what everybody calls me. I've seen you round here a lot, haven't I?"

"I come here a lot," Paul said, still wondering what she wanted to know.

"I saw you emptying the teapot up the garden the other night, didn't I?"

"You probably did," Paul agreed, wiping the pink Window-lene off in big circles.

The woman came out on to the pavement a little more, and jerked her head towards the house. "That's Mrs Maxwell in there, isn't it?"

Paul stopped work and faced her. "Don't you know?" he asked rudely.

"Well, I go out to work, you know! I'm only here in the afternoons, and I got a family. I see her in the garden some-times—but she keeps herself to herself, don't she?"

"She gets rheumatism," Paul said. "She doesn't move about much when it's bad."

"Well, it's not my fault, is it, love!" The woman waited a little while, until he scrubbed less ferociously at the window. "Come to see her a lot, don't you?"

"Why don't you start keeping count?" Paul asked.

"You do a lot for her, don't you?" the woman said, nodding at the window.

Paul turned on her again, holding the bottle high by his head, as if he might throw it at her. "She's my gran," he said. "Nothing wrong with helping my gran, is there?"

"All right, love, all right, no need to be nasty, is there?" The woman's face turned vixenish. "I lent her some sugar once, you know." And she slammed back into her house. She left Paul feeling distinctly uneasy.

The first sign that things couldn't last came on a Friday afternoon. When Paul's class returned to their form-room to be dismissed, his form-teacher handed Paul a note addressed to his parents. Walking home with Mike and Tony, Paul opened the note with his thumb and read it. It said:

"Dear Mr and Mrs Mentor, Could we make an appointment to meet? I am concerned about Paul, and would like to have a talk with you about him. I don't know if you are aware of it or not, but Paul has been very frequently absent from school during the past few months. He has nearly always had a note, signed by you, excusing him for headache, stomach upset, 'flu, cough, cold, etc., but it is not unknown for such notes to be forged! I am sure you understand our desire to clear this matter up. So if one of you, preferably both of you, could 'phone the school and make an appointment, or just drop in one Tuesday afternoon, soon, I would be very grateful. Yours faithfully, E. Wickan, Deputy Headmaster."

"Oh heck," Mike said, as he read the note over Paul's shoulder. "I told you you'd never get away with it, all that waggin'. What'll your Mom and Dad say?"

"Nothing," Paul said thickly. "They won't get it. I shall rip it up."

"Oh come on, Paul," Tony said. "You won't get away with it. He'll want an answer to that, Wickan will. He might go and see your Mom, and what then?"

"Nothin'," Paul said, a wonderful idea growing in his head. "I shall write a note saying all that stuff about headaches and stomach upsets is true, and sign it from me Mom."

"Oh Paul!" Mike said, in horror. "Come on! You must be mad. What if they find out?"

"They won't find out," Paul said.

"You must be round the twist."

"Where d'you go anyway?" Mike asked. "When you play the wag. Where d'you go?"

"There's this big, sexy blonde lives along the Oakham Road——" Paul began, a dreamy look coming into his eyes, but Tony took hold of the nape of his neck and squeezed hard. "Oh ar, we've heard that one before. Where d'you go? Over the fields?" There was a place, in the fields, where some fourth years had made a very comfortable dug-out, where they hid when wagging.

"No," Paul said. "I just go around. Up the town. Pictures sometimes. You know. I go to the park 'times."

"Christ," Tony said. "I'd rather come to school."

"I think there must be summat in this big blonde," Mike said. "He's never around on a night now, is he?"

"No, he ain't. Not a *big* blonde though."

"Yes she is," Paul said. "A great big fat blonde—corr!" He bent backwards as if supporting great weight, and made a loop of his arms in front of him.

"She must be kinky," Mike said.

"Paul, you want to be careful," Tony warned. "You'll be coming in suffocated one of these days."

"You comin' out tonight though, Paul?" Mike asked. "Eh? Phelpsie, he's got this old canoe an' he's takin' it on the canal tonight. He might let us have a go."

Paul's face took on an abstracted look. "Ah—no, not tonight,"

"Why not, Paul?"

Paul ripped the letter and envelope crisply in half. "Don't feel like it."

"Remember," Tony said, with a sneer, "he's got his fat blonde waiting for him. Am you courtin' or summat, Paul?"

"Don't be daft!" Paul said angrily. "I gotta go visitin' with me Mom."

"Visitin' who?" Tony rapped back.

"Me aunt!"

"Aunt who?"

"Mind your own business!"

"You'm courtin'," Tony said. "It's that buck-toothed spotty wench lives next door to you, ain't it? No wonder he don't want to admit it! He's blushin'—look—it's right!"

Paul was filled with sad, painful anger, on his own behalf, and on that of the shy, abused girl who lived next door. Tears came to his eyes as he drove his foot into Tony's shin as hard as he could. Tony began to hop, clutching his leg, swearing. Mike laughed.

Furious at being unable to knock them all out with a blow, like Mohammed Ali, Paul ran in and tried to kick Tony's supporting leg out from under him. It looked like a girl's way of fighting, he thought, but his fists were tiny compared to Tony's and he couldn't make much impact in the heroic style.

Tony stopped hopping when he saw him coming, and dodged a step or two backwards before stooping to rub his shin again. "You've crippled me, you little bastard!" It was even more shaming that Tony wouldn't hit him back.

"He's a bloody mad 'un!" Tony said loudly. "D'you see him go for me? What have I done?"

Mike was still laughing, incredulous and doubled-up. Paul running in like that—Tony's face—it was like a film.

Paul turned and left them, running out of the school grounds and up on to the bridge. There he remembered to rip the letter into tiny pieces, showering them over the parapet on to the road beneath.

Chapter Seven

Paul half-walked, half-ran in long, stamping strides, trying to keep to the rhythm of a tune that played in his head. Again and again he passed from strips of grey darkness to pools of grainy light beneath lamp-posts. There were few people about, it being a lonely road, fields on one side, a golf-course on the other, just one or two posh little houses, and the lamps widely spaced. It was late too, half-ten his watch said. Not so late as he usually was, because Mrs Maxwell had gone to bed early, at a quarter to ten. Well, it had been a tiring day for her.

They had gone to the park and done some shopping, and had then gone on to the pictures to see Walt Disney's *Sleeping Beauty*. It was the first day Paul had taken off from school for weeks, but a Walt Disney cartoon was too much temptation. He couldn't ask his friends to see it with him and hold up his head again, so he had skipped school and gone to see it with Mrs Maxwell, who "ahhed" and "oohed" all the way through, and said, "Isn't it wonderful what they can do these days?" Paul disapproved of the cuteness and sentimentality, but it was the drawing and animation he had come to see. Disney was the best for that. He would get very excited and pull at Mrs Maxwell's sleeve, saying, "It's like real people! Look at that movement! It's perfect—how in the name of God did they manage that?"

The last stretch of the lane joined a cross-roads. On the corner opposite was a big pub, called "The Gallows" because there used to be a gallows-tree close by, or so local legend said. Paul crossed the road towards it. On the car park, in the orange light from the lamps, a gang of lads on motor-bikes rode in circles and revved-up. One called to him, he thought, but even if he'd been certain, he would have ignored them. As he stepped out across the entrance of the car park they came roaring past him in a swirl of dust and fumes, noise of engines and shouting. One shoved a screwed-up bundle of fish and chip papers into his face. They nearly ran him down, and sped off with animal guffaws and yodellings. He threw the fish and chip papers after them, but didn't call out anything. Anything he called them they would take for a compliment.

He carried on down the hill, turning into his own street, and coming eventually to his own house. He opened the door with the key from around his neck, took off his jacket and threw it over the old pram in the front room. Feeling thirsty, he went along the hall and got a bottle of milk from the fridge, poured himself a glass. Years ago Mal had told him that milk contained radioactivity, and made you thirstier if you drank it when you were thirsty. Even at ten he had thought: Mal showing off again, but every time he'd had a drink of milk since, he'd thought of the radioactivity and wondered if it would really make him thirstier. He never remembered to notice.

He supposed, while he was drinking, that he might as well look in on the family. Was it only last week that he'd spoken to his mother as they'd passed in the hall? Smiling to himself, he opened the living-room door.

As soon as he went in, he knew something was wrong. They both looked at him.

"What time d'you call this?" his mother asked. "Turn the set down, Horace." And his father turned the television sound down straight away.

"What's up?" Paul asked.

His mother was nervous and snappish, whipping her

cigarette from her mouth and slapping it at the edge of her ash-tray. "What time do you call this to come in?"

Paul looked at his watch. Nearly a quarter to eleven. He'd often come in later and she hadn't bothered. "What?" he said.

"And where do you think you've been?"

"Out," Paul said. He reached behind him for the door-knob.

"Come back here. You're not going anywhere. Come on, right into the room, if you please, where we can see you." Her face was growing red and her voice harsh-edged. Paul went to the settee, and stood behind it, leaning on the back, like a prisoner in the dock.

Mrs Mentor's anger had obviously been stewing in her for some hours, and she had some control over it. She wasn't going to jump up and make undignified swings for him, which he could dodge. "What's this I hear?" she began, and paused for a drag at her cigarette.

Oh God, Paul thought. She knows I've been playing the wag. There'll be Hell to pay.

"What's this I hear about you visiting your gran?"

"Eh?" Paul said, in true astonishment. His father's parents resided in Top Church graveyard, his mother's at Rood End cemetery. He could remember very little about any of them.

"I met Mrs Grover today. 'I been hearing about your Paul,' she ses. 'How good he is to his gran.' " She looked at him, waiting for an explanation.

"She must be mad," Paul mumbled.

"What?"

"I don't know what she was on about."

"She seemed to know what she was on about. Went on about you running errands and carrying shopping, and what not, for your gran. I want to know what you been up to, young man."

Paul slid a look sideways, to see what his father was making of all this. His father had turned around in his chair with his back, almost, to the television screen. His hands were loosely clasped together, he stared at the carpet.

"I don't know anything about it," Paul said.

"Mrs Grover said it was you, running errands for your gran," Mrs Mentor slapped her hand hard on the table. "Now *what* is this all about?"

"I dunno," Paul said truculently. "How d'you expect *me* to know?"

Mr Mentor rumbled in his throat to clear it, raised his heavy head and said, "Answer your mother."

He sounded as if a string had been pulled, and the words ground out mechanically, but Paul watched him nervously. "Honest. I *don't* know. I don't know any Mrs Grover. She must have made a mistake."

Mrs Mentor smiled thinly, in triumph. "Mrs Grover knows you, though. 'I been livin' next door to this old lady for years,' she ses to me, 'and never knowed it was your mother.' 'My mother's been dead eight years,' I ses. 'Oh then,' she ses, 'it must be your husband's mother your Paul visits.' "

Mr Mentor raised his head again. His mother had died when he was eleven. The look Paul gave him was even more nervous.

" 'He's there in the afternoons sometimes,' Mrs Grover said. 'He's always there,' she ses. 'Till ever so late at night.' And when I said it couldn't be your gran, she said you'd told her it was. Now Paul, what have you been doing? I want to know. Who is this you'm goin' to visit? Come on, I want an answer——"

"Give him a chance then," Mr Mentor said, and then turned his blank, square face towards Paul.

Paul stood with his hands on the back of the settee, staring between them at the fireplace. After a minute he began to bite at his lower lip. And still they waited. His mind fell into a state of scrambled panic.

He didn't want to tell them about his old lady, because she

was nothing to do with them, and anyway, if he told them about her, he might have to tell about the days off, and the rug, and the slippers, and the stolen dinner-money and the notes signed in their name. . . .

Mrs Mentor's temper boiled over, and she jumped up, leaning across the settee with her hand outstretched to slap. "If I don't get an answer in a minute, my lad, I'm going to give you such a hidin'."

Mr Mentor shook his head. "Else," he said, "sit down, for God's sake."

"Oh, it's all right for you, you ain't responsible for——"

"Else. You'm gettin' nowhere. Now sit down. Paul—come here." And when Paul hesitated, "I said, come here."

Paul shuffled slowly around the settee to stand by his father's chair. "You ain't on trial," Mr Mentor said, "sit down." He slipped a thick arm about Paul's waist and pulled him on to the arm of the chair. His head was on a level with Paul's shoulder. "Now then; what's all this about?"

Paul was aware of the motive behind this sudden affection; he wasn't fooled. But he saw too that he was going to have to reveal all, and his father seemed to be offering better terms than his mother.

"There's this old lady named Mrs Maxwell," he said. "I been visiting her."

"That wasn't so bad, was it? You been visitin' an old lady. What's all the row about then?"

"He can visit her, he didn't have to——" Mrs Mentor said.

"Else, Else. Here's your mother, Paul, frothin' at the mouth—I dunno why. . . .?"

He left the sentence hanging, his calm, heavy face attentive and waiting. After one quick glance, Paul couldn't look at him, but stared past his ear at the shifting grey forms on the television screen.

"She's mad 'cos I been playin' the wag."

"*Have* yer?" Mr Mentor asked unbelievingly.

Paul was irritated that his father was taking such a whimsical tone. "Wednesday afternoons," he said. "Lots of times. And Thursdays. Lots of times."

"Is that all?" Mr Mentor asked. "Is that all?" he asked his wife, then shushed her before she could speak. He tightened his arm around Paul, rocking him. "Tell us about this old lady," he prompted gently.

He made all Paul's worries look small and silly.

"She has rheumatism," Paul said and, for the first time, looked fully into his father's face. There were his own brown eyes, but older, quieter, resigned and humorous. "She can't move about much. I make tea for her."

"Mmm?" said his father.

"I get her shoppin' for her—and that," Paul added lamely. He tried to think of something else he did. Surely not so little. It all seemed so pointless.

"I take her to the pictures." A quick look at his father again. "On Wednesday afternoons." He looked over his shoulder at his mother's flushed and angry face. "And I washed her clothes with the dinner-money you give me—at the launderette —instead of stoppin' dinner." He knew that if he didn't confess every little sin now they would only turn up later, seeming much bigger and blacker alone.

"You been doing all this, have you?" his father asked. "When?"

"Nights," Paul said. "Weekends."

"And days an' all from what I hear," his mother said acidly.

"Days an' all," Paul mumbled.

"Well, I never knowed," Mr Mentor said, rubbing his nose from side to side with a wet sound. "First I've heard of it. Why so hush-hush, me hero?"

Paul had no answer for that one. He looked at the carpet and said nothing.

Mr Mentor sniggered. "I could understand you not wantin' us to know if you was visitin' some fat little blonde somewhere;

but not an old lady. Hey——" he dug Paul in the ribs, "—you sure it ain't a fat little blonde? Can I have her address? Eh?"

Paul didn't crack a smile, and Mrs Mentor was sourer than a lemon, so Mr Mentor took his arm from around Paul, and turned the television sound up again. He'd done his job. He'd got the story. Still, he kept one ear on the argument.

Paul stood up from his father's chair. He knew that his father was finished with the whole matter now, apart from curiosity as to how it would end. He hadn't been fooled. He'd only used his father as a spoke for his mother's wheel. Now he faced her with his hands in his pockets and his head tilted up, a pose of defiance and superiority. Mrs Mentor's eyes were bright and wide, her mouth pressed tight. She was dying to shout and rave and bawl him out, but his father's calm attitude had put an end to that.

"She must be a right un, this old lady, to encourage you to take time off from school, and steal the money I give you for your dinner. A *very* nice sort of person."

Paul sighed and looked at the ceiling. He supposed it was a good argument, one, anyway, that he wasn't going to try and answer. He was just glad that Mrs Mentor seemed more concerned over Mrs Maxwell's character than his truancy.

"Why keep her such a secret?" Mrs Mentor went on, flicking ash from her cigarette, an edge to her voice like a razor. "Is her too good for us? Am you ashamed of us, or something? You'd think so from the amount of time you've spent with us just lately."

Paul shifted his weight from one foot to the other, giving an impression of total boredom. Mrs Mentor smashed her cigarette in the ash-tray and screeched, "What d'you call her 'gran' for?"

Paul jumped at the suddenly loud voice and, caught off-guard, answered truthfully, "She's just like a gran."

Mrs Mentor's voice shook. "You had a gran of your own. What you want to go and find some old faggot out for——"

Paul reacted like a wet cat. "She's *not* an old faggot! She's—she's——"

"A nasty old woman!"

Paul was breathless. "You don't *know* that! You don't know anything about her! You don't——"

"I know the kind that'd set a kid to *steal* from his mother!"

Mr Mentor laughed, but whether at them or the television they couldn't tell.

Mrs Mentor fumbled for a cigarette while Paul fumbled for the answer that would crush her into the ground.

"I don't know," Mrs Mentor began again, talking around her cigarette as she struggled with a box of matches. "You can go round there and run errands and I don't know what, but you won't even put a kettle on here. You never do anythin' for me."

Paul had his answer. "Well, if you did half as much for me as Mrs Maxwell does, maybe I'd feel like doing summat for you."

She sat still, the cigarette dangling from her mouth.

Paul turned and left the room quickly, slamming the door.

Mr Mentor looked at his wife with sad amusement. "Else; Else."

Mrs Mentor pretended not to hear. She smoothed her skirt and lay back in her chair, dragging on her cigarette with narrow, cat's eyes.

Paul got up later than usual the next morning, at quarter to eight. He listened to the house, and it had that white silence which meant it was empty. He could always tell, just by listening, if the house was empty or not. If people were in it, even if they kept very quiet, the house seemed to breathe with them.

He washed and dressed, and went downstairs to the living-room. He lit the gas-fire, but that was as far as his energy carried him. He slumped on the settee with his hands between his knees, and was very miserable.

There didn't seem to be any one thing more than another to be miserable about. Everything was miserable. Everything.

He couldn't even think what.

When the door opened behind him he jumped and looked quickly round. It was his mother coming in with an armful of washing which she spilled on to the settee.

Paul disentangled himself from a sheet, and watched her balefully as she came around the settee in her short green housecoat, to get a cigarette from the coffee-table. She wore no shoes or stockings. "There was a pair of blue slippers round here," she said musingly. "Can't think what happened to 'em."

Paul wasn't on speaking terms with her, but curiosity was niggling him. He picked a pair of frilly knickers from his hair and said, "You'm going to be late."

"Oh, don't you worry about me, Sunny Jim."

"I ain't worried. I couldn't care less—Ain't you going to work, then?"

"No," said his mother. "I'm not." She took off the house-coat and threw it into her chair. She had a pink nylon slip on underneath. Turning to the mirror, she began to comb her hair. Paul sombrely studied the blue veins in the back of her yellowing, muscular thighs.

"Where you going?" he asked glumly.

"Wouldn't you like to know?" She came and bent over him, smelling of face-powder, and tobacco, and sweat, not like a mother at all. Mothers smelt of—well, he wasn't certain, but they shouldn't smell like *his* mother, of that he was sure. His mother said, "Get up, get up. You're sitting on my dress."

Paul got up and moved to one side, standing disconsolately in his shirt-sleeves, with his hands in his pockets. His mother found her dress from among the jumble, shook it out and pulled it over her hair. As her head appeared from the neck, she said, "Can you find my tights?" She said it as an order, not a request, to let him know his place.

Paul swung from the waist, looking round. From the floor at his feet, from among a sprawl of women's magazines, he picked up some grey, shrivelled things and held them aloft.

"They're Kath's," Mrs Mentor snapped. She found them herself. They were thrown over the back of the settee, and hidden by the washing. She sat down to put them on.

"Where you going?" Paul asked again, suspiciously.

Mrs Mentor stood up, pulling her tights up about her waist, wriggling into them. "I'm going to see that bloody old woman you took up with," she said.

A chord struck, Da-da! in Paul's head, as if in a television play or film. "What for? What you want to do that for?"

Mrs Mentor took her shoes from the coffee-table and slipped them on. She smoothed her dress and patted at her hair, and there she stood, a cool, neat, attractive woman. But she seemed to find it hard to answer him.

"I'm going to find out what kind of woman this is that my son's living with. Why else? I am your mother."

Paul stared blankly at her. Her words didn't mean anything to him. He struggled to understand what she had said, but it was like trying to walk when you were waist-deep in water.

"You don't know where she lives!" he said triumphantly.

"Don't I?" Mrs Mentor asked with a malicious smile. "Oh, don't I?" She turned away to the door, and Paul hurried after her.

"What're you going to do? What're you going to say to her?"

Mrs Mentor gave him one look over her shoulder, jerked the door open and went out into the hall.

"I can tell you what she's like," Paul said, following her. "You don't need to go—she's nice, quiet." He frowned, trying to think of qualities that would appeal to his mother. "She's *decent* and *respectable*."

"Oh yes," his mother said. "That's just the kind that keeps a kid away from school, and tells him to rob his own mother."

"She didn't, she didn't!" Paul yelled at her, but now their roles were reversed. She calmly buttoned up her coat and didn't seem to hear, even though he had shouted so loud that his voice had echoed off the ceiling upstairs. She turned to the door.

This was bad. This was very bad. It was like the farces where the man's in bed with his girl-friend and his wife comes home; or in the films where the burglar just has the safe open when the police arrive. It's funny in farces and films, but for real it's not funny. People get hurt, and that's never funny.

It was terrible that Mrs Maxwell might meet his mother.

"Mom, please don't go," he said, but he knew it was no good. The harder he tried to persuade her not to go, the more determined she became.

And then, her face concerned behind the smoke from her cigarette, she asked, "Paul; why don't you want me to meet her?"

Now they were on to those questions that people ask now and then that sound rehearsed; straight out of an American soap-opera; a question that didn't fit her at all, and completely threw Paul.

"I don't know," he said. He took his jacket from the pram in the front room. "I'm coming with you."

"You've got to go to school."

"Well, you should be going to work."

She shrugged. "I'm sure it makes no difference to me. But I shan't write you a note for school."

"You never did," Paul said. He ran back into the living-room to turn off the gas, and into the kitchen to lock the back door. His mother was gone when he got back. He slammed the front door shut and ran up the road after her.

They caught a bus because Mrs Mentor wasn't prepared to walk, and during all the ride, and all the walk uphill, they never spoke a word.

Paul stopped outside the shabby little door, and Mrs Mentor, standing very straight and holding her handbag in front of her, said, "Is this it?" Paul nodded. "Well—go on then—knock."

Reluctantly, Paul knocked on the door and went in. He went to the armchair by the fire, but Mrs Maxwell wasn't there. The fire was in the grate, a teapot and plate were on the table, so he knew she was at home and feeling sprightly. He went into the kitchen, and looked into the yard, but couldn't see her, so he came back to the main room, opened the stair-door and called, "Mrs Maxwell." There was no answer, but he stepped up, and vanished behind the stair-wall.

"Paul!" Mrs Mentor hissed. "Paul—come back!" But he was gone. Her hands twisted on the strap of her bag with embarrassment. She'd thought she'd brought him up better than to run wild in other people's houses.

Then she raised her eyes and, for a second, was shot straight into deep space.

The picture stretched across the wall: a brilliant ringed planet; a silver rocket; blue, green, red, depths of blackness.

Mrs Mentor had never seen a picture like it.

And now she saw other pictures, painted, crayoned, big and small, tacked all around the walls. She didn't care much for paintings or drawings, but she had never seen so many together in one room, and certainly not in the house of an old lady. There were some strange pictures which she didn't like at all; they disturbed her with their weird shadow effects and emptiness. Others of streets and houses she thought dull; she liked the portraits the best. One sketch she was sure was of Paul; perhaps this old lady was an artist. Others were of old women—it didn't seem to be the same person. And then, in the corner of a drawing of an old lady sleeping, she saw a signature. It was full and flourishing, obviously written with pride, and it read, P. A. Mentor: Paul Adrian Mentor.

Mrs Mentor stepped back to look at all the paintings with

astonishment. She had known that Paul could draw rather well, of course. His pockets were always full of pencil nub-ends when she came to wash his clothes; and he used to annoy his father by doodling Greek warriors in the margins of the newspapers. But she had never known him do anything like this.

She turned at the sound of feet on the stairs. Paul came down first, jumping off the bottom step and holding up his arm for someone behind him.

The famous old lady. She was small and dumpy, and leaned heavily on Paul's arm and shoulder as she carefully lowered one foot to the floor. Her face, as she peered at Mrs Mentor, was round and timid behind her glasses. "You're Paul's Mom, then?" she said, and Paul sighed. At least some of what he'd been telling her upstairs had sunk in.

"Paul," said Mrs Maxwell, "go and put the kettle on, love, and give your Mom a cup of tea."

Paul took the teapot and plate into the kitchen, but kept one ear cocked to the conversation.

Mrs Mentor drew herself up and clutched her handbag tighter. "Mrs Maxwell," she began, "I've come——"

"Look at this," Mrs Maxwell said happily. She stumped slowly across the room to one of the pictures. "Our Jeff started this, but he never finished it, so Paul finished it for me. Ain't it beautiful? And this," she said, moving along to another. "He done this of me. Oh, he is a clever lad, Paul is."

"Yes, I know—Mrs Maxwell——"

"He comes every day, you know, to see me. Every day. He looks after me, he does. Like a mother-hen. Ain't you, Paul?"

Paul smiled as he put clean cups on the table. The name no longer hurt; she was just teasing. He had set out the best cups, and fetched the milk in the jug, because he knew how Mrs Maxwell would want things done, and besides, he wanted to make her look better than his mother, who had milk-bottles and sugar-bags on *her* table. As soon as he could, he went back to the kitchen.

"Paul! Paul!" the old lady squeaked, in the nearest she could get to calling. Paul put his head in from the kitchen. "I got some cakes in the tin. Bring some plates." Paul gave thumbs-up and disappeared again. "He makes fires," the old lady said eagerly to Mrs Mentor. "He's a lovely boy. Do you know, he took all the cups down from the top shelf in the kitchen so I wouldn't fall getting 'em."

Mrs Mentor's eyes fell on the fluffy blue slippers the old lady wore, and her hands tightened again on her handbag. "*Did* he?" she said.

"Sit down, my love," Mrs Maxwell said. "Sit down and make yourself comfortable."

Mrs Mentor pulled a straight-backed chair out from the table and placed herself stiffly on it. "I will sit down, Mrs Maxwell. I want to have a word or two with you."

The old lady didn't hear. She was stooping slowly at a sideboard cupboard. "I hope you like home made cake. I made these just the other day, they'll still be fresh. I keep 'em in a tin."

Paul came in with the teapot. He had rolled up the brown rug from the kitchen and hidden it in the outside lavatory. With a clear conscience he ignored his mother, and put the pot down on the little cork mat.

"Paul," said the old lady, straightening slowly with the cake tin in her hands. "You haven't taken the plastic off."

Paul groaned.

"You'll never be a good husband," Mrs Maxwell said.

Paul took the teapot and cups and plates from the table and put them on a chair while he took off the plastic cloth, then quickly put the things back on the table. He held out his hands for the cake tin. "I'll open that. You go and sit down."

"I'm not sitting down when I've got a visitor. You go and fetch them teaspoons you forgot."

"You gotta sit down though," Paul said, backing off towards the kitchen. The old lady smiled idiotically at him.

"Mrs Maxwell——" Mrs Mentor began again, with politeness as bright and cold as the white china teacups.

But Paul was back, a bunch of teaspoons clinking in his hand. "I'll open the tin, I'll pour the tea," he said. "You go and sit down."

He hasn't looked at me once since he came downstairs with her, Mrs Mentor thought.

"It's my house," Mrs Maxwell said, almost giggling. "I'm hostess," she said, and did giggle.

Paul took her arm and pulled. "Come on, come on and sit down. I'll bring you your tea."

"Stop it, stop it," she said. She was trying to open the tin, but he was swaying her. Paul reached over and jerked off the lid. Then he grabbed a cake from inside, and stuffed half of it into his mouth.

The old lady watched him proudly and fondly, and asked, "Nice?"

Paul nodded, chewing hard. "Best you ever made," he said breathlessly.

Mrs Maxwell ruffled his hair up from his brow, stroking it back and leaving it standing on end. Paul put his arm around her waist and tugged. "Come on, sit down, come on."

They both stared in surprise when Mrs Mentor began to cry.

First her face screwed up, very ugly. She tried to straighten it, and, when she couldn't, turned half away. She made a croaking sound, and another. She couldn't stop.

Paul stood and watched her with indifferent interest, as you do an accident when no one you know is involved.

But Mrs Maxwell went hobbling around the table to put an arm about her, saying, "Oh dear, oh dear! Oh dear me. What can the matter be? Aren't you feeling well, my love?"

Paul almost laughed, but went on watching. He thought his mother was putting on a good act, but the dialogue was corny.

"Don't cry, love, don't cry. What's the matter? Have you

got a headache? Do you want an aspirin? Paul—pour your mother a cup of tea."

Obediently, Paul lifted the pot and poured tea into three cups. Mrs Mentor glared at him, and said angrily, "He does everything for you, don't he? He never does *anything* for me! He never does anything in his own house."

Paul glanced up at her for a second, then added milk to the cups.

"He never runs errands for me," Mrs Mentor said wildly. "He never asks *me* to sit down." Her face folded in again, squeezing out more tears. "He never done *me* any pictures!"

Paul was shocked to find himself on the end of an accusing stare from his old lady. He held a spoonful of sugar over a cup. "It's not *my* fault!" he said. "If I'd shown her a picture she wouldn't have been bloody interested."

Mrs Mentor had her elbows planted on the table, her fists clenched at her face. "You never *showed* me a picture!" she wailed.

"You wouldn't have been interested," Paul said. "You never was interested in anythin' I did. You never listen."

"Paul," Mrs Maxwell said. "You shouldn't speak of your mother like that. *Of course* she's interested in you. She's your *mother*. She *loves* you."

Paul flushed. He pointed dramatically at Mrs Maxwell. "*You'm* interested in me." And at his mother. "*She's* not."

Then Mrs Mentor arose in wrath. "You ungrateful little bleeder!" she shouted across the table. "After all I done for you."

"Fed me and clothed me," Paul said flatly. "Make out a bill and I'll pay you back when I start work."

Mrs Mentor swelled. "If it wasn't for me, you wouldn't be here!"

"I didn't think you'd noticed I *was* here!"

"Oooooh!" Mrs Mentor cried, and started round the table. "Just wait till I get you home, my lad."

Paul retreated smartly around the table in the opposite direction, chivvying Mrs Maxwell before him to the hearth. "Sit down," he said, and she sat down in her armchair, out of the way. Still backing off, Paul said to his mother, "I think you should go home and leave Mrs Maxwell in peace."

His mother gasped. "*Don't* you tell me what to do!"

"You'd think you wouldn't need tellin', if you had anythin' about you!"

Mrs Mentor stopped dead in the middle of the room, and raised her hands to her head. "See?" she wailed to Mrs Maxwell. "He don't care. He don't care for me a bit!"

"Aah," Mrs Maxwell said. She heaved herself out of her chair and went to put her arms about Mrs Mentor. "Paul, you are a bad boy."

Paul didn't know whether to laugh or cry. "What about me? What about *me*? She don't care for *me* a bit. She was going to thump me. What about me?"

"I don't care for him, he ses," Mrs Mentor sobbed. "I could have stopped home and had an easy life, but no. I went out to work so we'd have more money and he never wanted for anything."

"Oh Paul," Mrs Maxwell said, over his mother's shoulder. "Oh Paul, you are a bad boy."

Paul couldn't understand it. She was his old lady. His, his, his. All that he'd done for her. His old lady. "What you on *her* side for?"

"I'm on your side," she said. "She's your mother."

Well, that was a very simple view of it, Paul thought. But then, his old lady was simple. He was losing her. Losing her to his *mother*.

"All right, all right," he said. "I'm sorry!" He shoved into their embrace, as he'd shoved between his mother and father when a very small child. "I'm sorry, I'm sorry!"

"That's right, love," Mrs Maxwell said. "I'm sure your Mom knows you didn't mean it."

"Oh, I'm so relieved," Mrs Mentor said. "I thought he'd got himself mixed up with somebody no good. I thought he wasn't telling me the truth."

"I know, I know, love," Mrs Maxwell crooned.

Everything was love and peace. Mrs Maxwell sat on one side of the hearth, and Mrs Mentor sat on the other. Out poured all Mrs Mentor's life. Back came all Mrs Maxwell's. And the neighbours. And the newspapers. And croonings, and platitudes, and complacencies.

Paul sat below it all, on a footstool at Mrs Maxwell's feet. He ate her cakes and brooded. He had lost to his mother.

Mrs Maxwell's attention was no longer centred on him. If he jumped up to get her another cup of tea, it didn't matter. He was put to one side now. Bloody women.

The hours seemed endless until Mrs Mentor was saying, "I hate to go, I really do, but I shall have to get his tea—something light, you know. Come on, Paul—can I come and see you again? I will, me free afternoon. You'll have to come to us for dinner one night. Come on, Paul."

"I want to stay here," Paul said sullenly. Perhaps he could make up lost ground when she was gone.

"You go with your Mom, Paul," Mrs Maxwell said.

Paul stood up immediately, and turned to the door. That was it. Life's last, harsh lesson. The final rejection. He would never come to see her again. He wondered whether to ask her for the space-ship picture back. . . .

No, let her keep the pictures. He would never set foot in the house again. Smartly he opened the door.

He didn't join in the effusive goodbyes, but stood by, moody and silent, until they had done. He followed his mother down the road, listening to her chatter, but never answering.

"If I'd known that was who you was visitin', I'd never have worried. What a lovely old soul! Paul, why did you have to go and skip school like that? You might have got her into trouble. I don't know what I'm going to do with you. I'll get you a box

of paints for your birthday. Would you like that? Oh look—
daffodils."

They were in a box outside a grocer's shop near the bus-
stop. Six pence a bunch. Mrs Mentor went in and bought
three.

"Aren't they lovely?" she kept saying, as they went on to
the bus-stop. "I love daffodils. They're the first flower of
spring."

Oh God, thought Paul. Where's the violins?

"They're such a lovely colour. It always makes me happy to
look at daffodils."

God preserve us, Paul thought. Who wrote this script?

"I shall take Mrs Maxwell some when I go to see her next."

Oh go on, go on, rub it in, Paul thought.

She kept on rubbing it in during the bus-journey home.
How she'd enjoyed the chat, how the poor old soul must be
very lonely; how his father could fetch her to their house in
the side-car of his bike, to watch the telly and have a bite to
eat—and on, and on, and on.

Paul let them into the house with his key, wandered into the
living-room, and sat in a miserable heap on the settee. Mrs
Mentor laid the flowers on the coffee-table while she took her
coat off. She came back into the room and fidgeted about.

"I'm sure my blue vase was in here," she said.

She came round to the mantelpiece, and placed a finger
carefully on the shelf near the shell-covered bottle. "I'm sure
that vase was there. Paul, have you seen my blue vase? Paul?—
Paul?"

Paul was sitting up straight on the settee, a beatific smile
spread over his face. He'd just realized. . . .

He'd just realized why his mother had been so angry about
Mrs Maxwell, why she'd gone to see her, why she'd cried. . . .

She was jealous . . . like he was . . . oh well. If he could play
his mother for money, and have Mrs Maxwell coming to the
house like his mother had said . . . it'd be like having a gran.

"Paul!" his mother yelled. "Where's—oh blow! Go and answer the door, will you?"

Someone was knocking at the door, a firm, polite tapping. Paul went down the hall to answer the door.

He got a shock. On the step stood Mr Wickan, his Deputy Headmaster. "Hello, Paul," said Mr Wickan with a smile. "Is your mother in? I've come to see her about some letters she wrote to me. May I come in?"

Paul sighed and stepped back. "I suppose so. Her's found out the blue vase's gone anyway."